Madeleine M

Superheroes in Sterkstroom

Nina

Tess

Bonnie

Mila

Indigo

Arno

Jimmy

Madeleine Muller

Books by Madeleine Muller

#Abancedi Series
Teenage Superheroes in the Eastern Cape

Nina's Nest
The Mystery of the Lost Horse

1 Runnin' on the Flats
2 Dimbaza Divine
3 On the rocks at Mdumbi
4 Superheroes at Sterkstroom

Available on Kindle - scan QR code:

Knights of the Round Earth Series

Pool of Sorrows
Vlinderslaagte
The Knights of the Round Earth
The Sun Bearers
Nandipha's Secret
Mr Taylor's Project

Superheroes in Sterkstroom

Written for Ron & Benji
2022

Indigo

Madeleine Muller

The moral right of the author has been asserted.

All characters and events in this publication, other than those clearly in the public domain, and any resemblance to real persons, living or dead, is purely coincidental.

First publication: November 2022

All rights reserved.
No part of this publication may be reproduced, stored in a retrieval system, or transmitted, in any form or by any means, without the prior permission by Dr Madeleine Muller.

Cover design by Benji Muller

ISBN: 9798365862739

#Teensuperhoes #LGTBQIA+ #enby
#EasternCape #YoungAdult #T1DM

Superheroes in Sterkstroom

Probably the last sound heard before the Universe folded up like a paper hat would be someone saying, "What happens if I do this?"

— Sir Terry Pratchett, Interesting times

"It was so loud and so deep, it wasn't really sound at all, just something that turned the air hard and then hit you with it."

— Terry Pratchett, The Bromeliad trilogy

Madeleine Muller

Superheroes in Sterkstroom

A word about pronouns

In this story we introduce a new character, Indigo, who identifies as non-binary, which is neither male or female. Which means the usual gender specific pronouns, he / she, would not necessarily be appropriate.

The most popular pronoun for a non-binary person is the singular they / them. The singular they/ them was often used in old Shakespearean English, but is still common in our language when using a gender neutral term e.g. someone / anyone / a child etc.
Examples: *There is someone at the door. Ask **them** what they want.*
*Help your child to put on **their** shoes.*
*Ask anyone and **they** will tell you.*

There are also a range of neo-pronouns that are becoming increasingly popular. In the chapters that are told from Indigo's point of view, I have used the neo pronouns ne/ nem/ nir.

Ne (rhymes with he/she): ***Ne*** identifies as non-binary
Nem (rhymes with them); Why don't you tell ***nem*** about it
Nir (rhymes with near): He liked ***nir*** name.

Ne went to the market with nir friends who love nem.

It's been fun exploring gender neutral pronouns in my writing. I hope you enjoy it as much as I did.

If you have a family member or friend that is transgender or non-binary and are interested in finding out more: This 45 minutes webinar covers the latest medical & scientific knowledge on transgender and gender diverse people and how family and friends can best support them.
https://youtu.be/kTtbzQ8q2ao

Madeleine Muller

Superheroes in Sterkstroom

Indigo

CHAPTER 1: *Indigo*

Surely in a population of seven billion people, ne was not the only one?

Indigo yawned and and clicked another link. Webpage after webpage flew past nir screen. These shotgun searches every night had become a bedtime habit, although the chances of a hit was seeming more and more improbable as the weeks passed.

It was a hot muggy Tshwane night, with a thunderstorm looming. Indigo checked the time at the bottom of the screen. It was past eleven pm on a Saturday night and ne was sitting in nir bedroom on the top floor of nir family's double storey house in the quiet suburbs of Centurion. Nir parents had gone to bed early, believing ne was busy with one of nir matric assignments.

But nope. Indigo was travelling the net and as usual, Google was clogged with useless rubbish. Maybe it was time to go to bed.

And then, an unexpected find....

Three words were highlighted on the opening page of the *TrueHeroes* website: 'Superheroes' and 'South Africa.'

No. Bloody. Way!

Indigo tried not to get excited. Most blogs on superheroes were either fiction or scams. Ne clicked on the article link, and a page of some foreign language rolled over the page. Indigo checked the top corner. No option for an English translation, but that would not be a problem. Scrolling to the bottom ne discovered the page was Indonesian.

Indigo opened another link and found the Indonesian news channel. The news reporter was, it seemed, reporting on a hurricane off the Philippine coast. Indigo listened for a few minutes and let the Indonesian wash over nemself.

And then - ne *shifted*.

When Indigo was 14 ne discovered that ne had the ability to shapeshift (ne called it *shifting* for short). It had been both wildly exciting and maddeningly strange. A skill ne didn't feel able to tell anyone about, nor could adequately explain. There had been no reason for it, and for all Indigo's searching, ne had never found anyone else with the same extraordinary gift, or any other superhero gift for that matter.

At first, learning to shapeshift had been hard and ad hoc, but these days making the jump was effortless, and ne could control how much of nemself ne wanted to shift at any one time. To understand a piece of foreign script, ne only had to shift nir thinking, as long as ne could find an example of the original language. In this case, the news reporter gave an an example of Indonesian Indigo could shift into.

The Indonesian dialect changed to English... or perhaps Indigo's brain had changed to Indonesian? Indigo had no idea how this shapeshifting worked, and who cares... Translating scripts had certainly been one of the more interesting ways to use nir power.

Quickly ne clicked on the article, which was now easy to read.

The journalist was reporting on an interview with a guy called Karief, living in Bali, one of the Indonesian islands. Karief worked in a shop as an IT guy or something, but in this article, he was interviewed about his adventures during a shipwreck off the coast of South Africa.

Indigo stopped reading and frowned.

A shipwreck on the east coast. That sounded familiar....

Ne continued reading.

In the article, Karief claimed that he had been rescued by a couple of extraordinary superhero twins, although he was maddeningly vague in the article about what kind of superpowers they supposedly had. The story was clearly narrated by some twenty-something cis-gendered male, who focused on how hot the girls were rather than what the hell had actually happened.

Indigo grunted in irritation.

Completely unhelpful.

Maybe looking up that shipwreck would help?

Quickly ne tried another search - this time for recent shipwrecks off the coast of South Africa. Ne was sure ne had heard something about a shipwreck in the Eastern Cape last year…

Sure enough, several links lit up. Indigo clicked on the top one and was so excited that it took nem a couple of seconds to realise why ne couldn't understand a word of the article.

Your brain is still in Indonesian, bro!

Quickly ne shifted back to English, and there it was. An article in the *Daily Dispatch*, a local South African, East London based newspaper. At the top of the front page was a photograph of two young men with their arms around each other's shoulders. One was the Indonesian youth, Karief, and the other was a beautiful brown-skinned boy, identified as Dawie Stuurman in the caption. The South African youth was tall and thin, his hair shortly shaven, with two small lightning bolts shaved into the sides.

Indigo quickly scanned the details, uninterested in the story of the illegal Indonesian fishing vessel and how it ended up on the rocks near the small Wild Coast village of Mdumbi.[1]

But there was nothing about a spectacular set of twins. It was all about Karief and Dawie, the hero of the day.

Indigo sighed. Another dead end. Ne re-read the article one more time and was struck by one of the comments.

The Daily Dispatch had previously featured the story of Dawie Stuurman and friends, who solved the mystery of the illegal cigarette poisoning fiasco in Keiskammahoek in April 2020, during the first COVID lockdown.[2]

One more try, Indigo thought as ne typed in 'Dawie Stuurman' and 'Keiskammahoek' into the search bar.

---

[1] See 'On the Rocks at Mdumbi'

[2] See 'Dimbaza Divine'

Madeleine Muller

And bingo!

The article was on page seven, and this time the Dispatch had a colour photograph of a group of six teenagers of different ages.

Immediately, Indigo's eyes were drawn to the two girls flanking that boy, Dawie, from the shipwreck article. The one on the left was a black girl, her skin the pitch-dark black of Eastern Africa. She was gorgeous. Her head had been recently shaven, the hair just starting to grow out. Indigo rubbed nir hands over nir own short, pitch-black hair. Ne had not been brave enough to shave all of it off yet. According to the subscript, the black beauty was called Mila. She looked straight at the camera with a gaze unafraid and slightly insolent.

But the strange thing was Mila's twin sister, Bonnie, for this girl's skin was as white as snow. The white girl was more slightly built than her voluptuous black sister, with long silver hair with golden streaks. Pretty, in that Ice Queen kind of way. Different as they were, you could see the two girls were sisters. They had the same green eyes and the same regal bearing.

Mila and Bonnie.

Indigo's heart beat faster.

The other kids in the picture were three twelve-year-olds identified as Tess, Nina and Ryan. The first one was, apparently, the Mgidi twins' younger sister, but Indigo had no interest in the younger children.

Indigo cracked nir knuckles and got going. For the next hour, ne researched everything ne could about the 'Keiskammahoek affair' - there was more information on the twins than the shipwreck story - although nothing about any supposed superpowers. But that did not discourage nem. By the end of nir search, Indigo sat back with a smile.

This could be it.

There were all sorts of clues that there was more to all this than reported on in the newspapers. And usually, journalists like to embellish, not leave things out.

The story simply didn't add up.

It didn't explain how two fifteen-year-old girls had solved the mystery and had saved those people's lives. And there was the whole business with

Superheroes in Sterkstroom

Dawie Stuurman, when the three Mgidi sisters had saved his life during a gang incident in Hanover Park. [3] And the same vagueness in details.

Could this be it?
People like nem?
Right here in South Africa?

Indigo didn't know why it should matter, but ne was getting lonely. The initial isolation due to being *enby*[4] had been small-scale compared to being, for a better word, a bloody superhero. And being gender expansive had been getting better by the day since ne came out. Indigo had discovered a whole queer community out there to embrace nem with open arms.

No chat rooms for superheroes, though.

But Indigo had figured that if ne existed, surely there must be others. Isn't that what these crazy nightly searches had been all about?

For a moment, Indigo allowed nemself to be elated before the next question arose.

Now what?

You can't exactly call up some stranger and ask, "Hey, do you have any superpowers?"

Indigo looked again at the picture of the twins. Ne yawned.

All this contemplation was getting exhausting.

Time to go to bed and sleep on it.

Tomorrow ne could plan.

---

[3] See 'Runnin on the Flats'

[4] non-binary (gender identification pronoun they/them)

Madeleine Muller

CHAPTER 2: *Nina*

Thirteen-year-old Nina stepped back from the large triangular chicken tractor, her hand over her mouth to hide her smile. It was a beautiful winter's evening on *Hog's Hollow Farm*, and she had finally agreed to let her best friend, Ryan, have a go at catching *Captain Henry*, the magnificent but slightly crazed Silkie cockerel.

At 13 years of age, Ryan was all limbs, but this had not decreased his effervescent Tigger bounce everywhere he went. Right now, he was ensconced in the chicken tractor - a large contraption with an in-built coop that kept the chickens safe from predators but allowed them to be moved each day across the farm fields. Crouched on hands and knees, bum in the air, he looked like a puppy eager to play, but Captain Henry was ignoring him flat.

"He knows you are there, Ryan," Nina shouted helpfully from the side. "I don't think there is any point in creeping up on him."

The brown-skinned boy gave Nina a mock glare and, with pursed lips, gestured for her to *zip it*. Slowly he crept forward. The mission was simple - to catch Captain Henry and take him to his special designated coop in the horse food storeroom for the night. Nina's grandmother, Jenni, had only one requirement when she had agreed to adopt the chickens: no

Superheroes in Sterkstroom

early crowing. So poor Captain Henry was separated from his harem each night and removed safely from earshot.

With a dramatic jump, Ryan lurched forward, surprisingly light-footed, but Captain Henry evaded him effortlessly. Ryan ended up flat on his face as the Silkie cockerel flew gracefully over his head and landed on his buttocks, clucking in irritation.

Nina almost doubled over in laughter.

"*Blerrie hoenner*,"[5] Ryan cursed, lying on the ground, but he was also smiling. It was difficult to take chickens seriously.

Captain Henry had been the hardest work of the flock of silkie chickens but was coming on nicely. The poor things had been somewhat traumatised when their owner had suddenly died a few weeks prior. Alex, the local young petite blonde-haired vet, had called Nina for help one Saturday morning.

"Sorry, Nina, but we are a bit stuck. Do you remember Tant Sannie with the Silkies?"

Nina didn't remember the old lady very well, but she did remember her chickens. They had met Tant Sannie once at the agricultural show, an eccentric auntie living on a small holding in the nearby village of Hogsback. The old lady had been breeding Silkie chickens for decades and had been a formidable figure locally, with her Silkies consistently nabbing all the prizes. But the flock had been more pets than prize winners and had lived in the house with the old lady, with free rein over both home and yard.

Alex had explained, "Well, it looks like the old dear had a heart attack or something, and she passed peacefully in her sleep a couple of days ago. She only has a daughter in Cape Town, who has asked us to clear the chickens before she gets here. But we don't know what to do with them. They have lived in this house in Hogsback for their entire lives and were quite attached to Tant Sannie. I know chickens are not sentimental, but this lot seems completely out of control."

"How many in the flock?" Nina asked, her heart rate quickening. She had always wanted chickens. Not that they would ever replace her horses

---

[5] darn chicken

Madeleine Muller

or Aero, her dog, but you couldn't put a horse on your lap. And her grandmother, Jenni, would surely be happy for the eggs.

Alex sighed, "I don't know. One of the neighbours just called me to come and fetch them. I was wondering if you'd come up with me to Hogsback, and we can go and have a look. You can tell me how they are doing."

Although Nina had only just turned thirteen, Alex treated her like an equal and was no longer embarrassed to ask for the blonde-haired girl's help with the more complicated animal cases. Since discovering Nina's extraordinary talent [6] with animals, Alex had been only too happy to involve Nina as her animal translator, especially with creatures that were traumatised emotionally or needed special handling.

Nina had a gift - the ability to tune in to animals, figure out what was going on and communicate some basic thoughts to them. Nina's first case had been Aunt Jorita's ill dog and, more recently, Toast, the beautiful Palomino stallion that had been found lost in the forest [7] and was now a happy part of the family. But this would be the first time she would get up close and personal with chickens.

"I would love to!" Nina had replied. "Let me just check with Maria and Granny Jenni."

Maria was Ryan's mom and Jenni's carer. Nina's grandmother had been blind for over a decade, and although she was still quite independent, she still needed some help around the house. Maria drove her grandmother to the shops, sorted out basic chores and cooked the evening meal. Since Nina had come to live at Hog's Hollow at age ten[8], she had happily taken over the care of the dogs and the horses and helped Maria with the laundry every week. Maria loved Nina to bits and was like a second grandmother to her - and had been particularly enthusiastic about the idea of fresh eggs.

*

---

[6] See 'Nina's Nest'

[7] See 'The Mystery of the Lost Horse'

[8] See 'Nina's Nest'

Superheroes in Sterkstroom

Alex Had picked Nina up in her bakkie an hour later, and they headed up the steep Hogsback pass to the picturesque village of the same name, nestled amongst three hog-shaped mountains. High enough to occasionally get snow in the winter, Hogsback was a popular tourist village, and with its ancient forests and beautiful waterfalls, it had the mystical feel of fairy tales and adventure.

Tant Sannie's house was at the end of a windy gravel road, and Nina had shivered as they parked in the pot-holed driveway. The house looked dilapidated, and the yard had not had any care for years. The poor chickens had been stuck in the house since Tant Sannie's death, unable to fend for themselves.

As they got to the front door, Nina could already hear the squawking.

"The neighbour said she would leave the door unlocked," Alex said, "and that she had fed and given the poor things water, but I'm afraid not much more."

Nina nodded grimly. This suddenly did not feel that much like fun.

Alex carefully opened the door, and the stench hit them with a blast. Nina wrinkled her nose.

"Yuck. Chicken droppings are particularly foul," Alex said, and Nina laughed at the pun. "But at least that is all it smells of."

The front door led into a passage that stretched through the house, with doors leading off on each side to bedrooms, a living room, and the kitchen in the back.

And there were chickens everywhere!

Nina stood in the hallway and burst out laughing. There was nothing more comical than a Silkie chicken. Silkie chickens are covered in soft feathers - some black and some white so the overall impression was that the house was infested with living feather dusters. Their crowns were a puff of downy feathers, completely hiding their eyes, and their feet were ensconced in the same soft fluff. Cute, ridiculous and relatively small, they nevertheless preened around like nobility.

Alex shook her head, "Good grief. In all my years, I have never seen anything like it." There were chickens in the passage, on the cupboards, roosting on light fittings, preening in the bath and sitting on the taps. "I don't even know where to start."

Madeleine Muller

Apart from the stench, the house was a cacophony of squawking sounds and chicken claws running on wooden floors. With Alex and Nina's arrival, the noise intensified, and chickens soon poured out of every room to come and investigate.

"Are they hungry? Thirsty?" Alex asked Nina.

Nina found a spot not too covered in chicken crap and sat down. Soon she was surrounded by Silkies, some climbing on her lap and one fluttering up and landing on her head. She closed her eyes.

"I think they like you," Alex said.

"They are very tame," Nina replied. She went quiet, and Alex did not interrupt again.

Nina found that deep quiet within herself. The noise and the smell vanished, and she felt at peace. She opened her eyes. Right in front of her was one of the larger Silkies, a beautiful pitch-black cockerel. He had his head cocked to one side and was looking at her intently. She put out her hand, and he fluttered back out of reach, but some of the hens came to peck at her fingers.

"They are not hungry," Nina offered, "but they are confused. They are looking for their carer. The whole order of the flock has been disturbed, so they are struggling to settle."

Alex nodded, "Not very surprising. But they will get sick if we keep them in this mess. I think Tant Sannie used to let them out during the day, and they would come in to roost in the house at night. They don't seem in terrible shape, but they will need a safe place while we figure out what to do with them. Who on earth is going to want these lot?"

"Is that a hint, Alex?" Nina asked with a smile.

Alex smiled back, "Not a hint, a definite request. But there is a good thirty chickens here. What would your grandmother say?"

Nina shrugged, "It's only temporary. And I will look after them. I am sure Mr Sibeko can quickly build us a couple of coops."

"Excellent," Alex said. "Then that is settled. It should not be too hard to find them new homes. And if you are keen, you can choose a small flock to keep for yourself."

Superheroes in Sterkstroom

Nina nodded enthusiastically. The Silkies had already decided that she would make an excellent replacement for Tant Sannie and was ignoring Alex flat.

They had returned to Hog's Hollow, and Mr Sibeko, the head groom and Nina's friend, had enthusiastically embarked on the task of creating the chicken tractors. A couple of days later, Nina was suddenly in charge of an exotic flock of Silkie chickens. They had managed to sell most of them on Gumtree, but she had kept ten for herself, with Captain Henry, the only rooster.

*

Ryan tried another couple of jumps using his particular brand of stealth to catch the poor rooster but soon gave up and opted, instead, to run around in mad circles inside the chicken tractor, screaming at the top of his voice. But it was to no avail; Captain Henry evaded him easily. Nina was crying with laughter when she finally went in to help. Ryan glared at her.

"*Die duiwel homself,*"[9] he grumbled.

Nina just shook her head and smiled as she easily picked up the puffed-up rooster, "Take's one to know one…" she teased. Ryan threw a raspberry in reply.

"*Nee wat*[10]. *Hoenners*[11] are for eating, I say. Not for blerrie playing."

---

[9] The devil himself

[10] no

[11] chickens

Jimmy

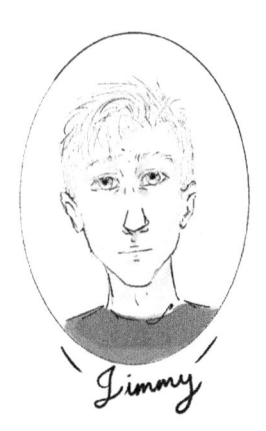

CHAPTER 3: *Jimmy*

Jimmy looked in the mirror that hung on the inside of his cupboard door and sighed. Why do they even manufacture ties that you have to knot? Surely they could get clever with the clip-on designs. He was on his third attempt, and his tie was even wonkier than the last two tries.

Blerrie useless he was. Useless at any of it.

"But you are only 19, my bra." That was what Arno would say. *"Nineteen-year-olds should not have any business in suits, ties, or multi-million rand deals."*

But thinking of Arno just made Jimmy's shoulders drop even lower. Jimmy lived in two worlds.

The first world was his own in which he was Jimmy, the only son of a wealthy magnate, ensconced in their white-tiered apartment on the steep Clifton banks in Cape Town overlooking the Atlantic Ocean. White privilege *in al sy glorie*,[12] destined for great things.

And then there was Arno's world, Arno who lived in a shack in a back yard on the Flats. Arno symbolised everything his dad sneered at - poor, brown and his own particular brand of queer. Although what exactly Arno was, Jimmy couldn't say.

---

[12] in all it's glory

Superheroes in Sterkstroom

The only thing he could say for sure about Arno was that Arno was his best friend, his person, the guy (or whatever Arno felt like showing up as) that had his back.

*

Things had been less complicated when they had still been at school. Arno had been poor enough and clever enough to get a sponsorship at King's College, the prestigious Cape Town school that each year "graciously" awarded two disadvantaged students a shot at a high-class education.

Jimmy still remembered that first day in Grade 8 when Arno sauntered into the classroom, his school blazer way too big on his narrow frame. He had looked so out of place. You could see he was a kid who did not always get a full three meals a day, his eyes always scouting for threats, fists in his pockets that probably did not even know hand cream existed. On a reflex, Jimmy had hid his hands under the desk, suddenly embarrassed about his soft, manicured nails. On the surface, the class had seemed well-behaved, but Jimmy had picked up the slight sneer, the barely disguised lifted eyebrow, and the shoulders angling away from the brown-skinned boy.

During first break, Jimmy had watched as Arno headed for the bench on the other side of the field. A kid with no lunch box and no context - out of place. Usually Jimmy was the quiet kid; the kid who liked to keep his head down and not stand out. Don't annoy the teachers, and don't draw out the other kids. Just quietly duck your way through life.

But on that day, Jimmy was suddenly unable just to watch. He crossed the field and sat next to Arno, zipping open his Woolworths lunch bag and taking out two perfectly crafted sandwiches. He handed one to Arno.

Arno looked at him in puzzlement as he took one, then gave Jimmy a big grin.

Madeleine Muller

"Why thank you, *liefling*[13]," he said, and Jimmy blushed. Arno had separated the two pieces of perfectly cut white bread and wrinkled his nose whilst inspecting its contents.

"*Jirre*, and what is this, *nogal?*"

Jimmy had cleared his throat with embarrassment, "Chicken mayonnaise. With bacon." And then as an afterthought. "It's great; you should try it."

"I'm not complaining, *skattie*[14]," Arno said quickly as he took a bite and then nodded with satisfaction. "*Hoenner en varkie oppie selle broodjie*[15]? Well, I nevir. *Blerrie* nice, though."

Jimmy had laughed, and suddenly, for the first time in his life, he had an actual friend. Or a BFF[16], as Arno would eventually call it.

*

But Arno wasn't here today to help him with his tie, although he would probably be in a state of hysterical laughter whilst trying to do it and still get it done perfectly.

"James! What the hell are you doing? We need to get going right this minute!"

Marthinus Brandt's voice echoed up the stairways of their Clifton mansion, and Jimmy felt his forehead moisten with sweat.

"I'm trying to tie this tie dad," Jimmy replied nervously.

"Just leave the damn tie," his father commanded.

He supposed his father would redo it anyway, even if it was perfect. Best just to get down there. They were meeting with Shoal Oil at 10.00 a.m. at the International Convention Centre in Cape Town about the Mangwa Reserve deal, and there would be hell to pay if he caused his esteemed father to be late.

Jimmy took a deep breath as he descended the stairs and headed out the door for his father's black Mercedes S580. He had been assigned the

---

[13] darling

[14] treasure

[15] chicken and pig on the same piece of bread

[16] best friend forever

simple task of taking down the minutes at this stupid meeting, but even that made him break out in a cold sweat. He repeated his breathing exercises all the way down the stairs, hearing his therapist's voice in his head, the back of his shirt already soaked through.

It was not a great start to his apprenticeship as a clerk in the Brandt Corporation.

CHAPTER 4: *Tess*

Tess deftly opened up the laptop and logged into her Zoom account. She smiled as both Ryan and Nina shook their heads in wonder.

"It's not so hard, guys. Geez, get with the times."

Tess, a little mixed-race girl with honey-brown skin, considered Ryan and Nina her best friends in the world, even though she lived on the coast, a good two-hours drive away. She tried to come to Keiskammahoek every opportunity she got, be it holidays or long weekends, and her parents made an effort to make it happen. Her grandmother, Jorita, used to live up here until the old lady passed away a year ago. Tess's mom had rented out her mom's old farmhouse and didn't mind coming through now and then to check on things.

Not that Tess would not also love to be at home with her older twin sisters, Bonnie and Mila, the coolest two sisters any kid could hope for. They were fun and awesome, and as only Tess and a couple of others knew, her sisters had superpowers.

When Tess first discovered the twins' awesome gifts when she was ten years old (the twins were fourteen at the time[17]), she knew their lives would never be the same again. And at first, they had included her in all

---

[17] See 'Runnin' on the Flats'

Superheroes in Sterkstroom

their adventures, but the girls were seventeen now and had started becoming interested in boys, gossip and make-up and stuff that thirteen-year-old Tess was still happy to ignore.

And she had had some pretty awesome adventures with Ryan and Nina, who she had been very happy to discover had her own superpower. Together they called themselves K.I.D. - the *Keiskammhoek Investigative Detectives* and they had already solved several legit cases!

And today, the K.I.D was being officially consulted!

Abongile, a passionate local conservationist, had sent Nina a WhatsApp asking if they could meet on Zoom. The large, passionate isiXhosa man no longer lived in Keiskammahoek but had joined the *Green Scorpions*, a section of the police force that investigated environmental threats such as poachers and illegal fishing and he was stationed somewhere inland. The three friends hadn't seen him since their adventure of finding Toast, Nina's beautiful Palomino stallion.[18]

Tess entered the Zoom link Abongile had sent and typed in the password.

"What do you think he wants, hey?" Ryan asked for the zillionth time, his eyes sparkling with excitement.

Tess sighed in exasperation, "Well, we will find out soon enough, Ryan. *Bietjie geduld seuntjie.*[19]"

Tess clicked the button to join with her computer's audio, and there was Abongile, large as life. His head was shaven, and he had grown a big bushy black beard. Behind him was a small and messy office.

"*Molweni, bantwana bam*[20]!" Abongile bellowed, a big smile on his face. Tess adjusted the screen to make sure that all three of them were nicely in frame, and they chorused back.

"*Molo*, Abongile," It was like being in school.

"*Heibo bantwana*, see how big you have become. What grade are you now?"

"We are in Grade 8, Abongile," Tess answered.

---

[18] See 'The Mystery of the Lost horse'
[19] A bit of patience boy
[20] Hello, my children

"High school already! *Hontsho*[21]! Proper teenagers now." The children laughed, already at ease.

"How can we help, Abongile?" Nina asked, prodded by Ryan, who was dying of curiosity.

Abongile smile vanished, "I am at a place here called *Mpangwa Nature Reserve*. *Niyayazi*[22]?"

The children shook their heads, and Abongile continued.

"It is an old run-down private game reserve just south of Sterkstroom, in the Joe Gqabi district. It covers about 5 000 hectares, a good area, and rich in game, especially small animals. They cater for tourists, but the lodge itself is not doing so well. COVID really made things hard. But that is not what worries me. What concerns me are the animals."

"The animals?" Nina asked. "All of them?"

Abongile ran his hand over his shaven head.

"Hayi, not all. But many of them. They are not right. But nothing consistent. Sicknesses, migrations, miscarriages and just odd behaviour. And in lots of different species. Nothing is clear. It makes no sense. We have tested the water and the soil and done autopsies on the carcasses we found left behind, but we haven't found anything. It's a mystery."

Tess' eyes widened, "And you need Nina to come and help?"

Abongile nodded, "I was speaking to Alex, and she reminded me of Nina's talents. I could really use another perspective here. But it would mean you would have to come out to *Mpangwa*. It is school holidays now, isn't it?"

Ryan clapped his hands together and whooped, "Ja, for sure, *bra*. K.I.D is ready for action."

Abongile looked slightly unsure. Tess suspected that the invitation had been for Nina only. But Nina understood this as well and asked,

"Would it be ok if Tess and Ryan also came, Abongile? Then it can be a bit of a holiday."

Abongile hesitated only for a moment before smiling widely, "Of course! It would be great to have all three of you rascals come and visit.

---

[21] congratulations

[22] Do you know it?

Superheroes in Sterkstroom

Alex is coming up, so she will be able to give you guys a lift. I'll ask her to arrange with all your parents."

All three children gave the thumbs up simultaneously, and Abongile laughed.

"*Kulungile ke.*[23] *Sobonana kamsinyane*[24]."

As soon as the meeting ended, Tess closed the screen, and the children screamed in excitement.

"And just when I thought it was gonna be a boring holiday, hey," Ryan joked, bouncing happily around the room.

Although with Ryan around, nothing ever gets boring, Tess thought.

And then Nina's phone rang. She looked at the number and pulled a face.

"Who is it?" Tess asked.

"Ag, I don't know. It is some cell number. Probably another person looking for Silkies. We have taken that advert off Gumtree, but I still get calls."

Nina sighed, opened the call and put it on speaker phone. Tess and Ryan were both insatiably curious, so it was best to let them listen in, or she would have to recount the whole conversation later, no matter how inane.

"Hello," Nina said.

"Hello," a beautiful husky voice said hesitantly on the other side, "My name is Indigo, and I am looking for someone called Nina…?"

---

[23] All right then

[24] We will see each other soon

CHAPTER 5: *Indigo*

Indigo could feel the sweat pouring down nir back. It had taken all nir courage that morning to dial the number, and it was pure luck that ne had picked up the Gumtree advert with Nina's cellphone number. It had been impossible to trace anything to the twins; this had been the only lead, the only possible way to make some sort of contact.

The voice of a young girl greeted upon answering, and Indigo introduced nirself, asking to speak to Nina. The voice on the other sounded irritated.

"Hello, this is Nina speaking. I'm afraid all the Silkies are gone." For a moment, Indigo was confused, and then ne remembered the advert. Of course, the girl was selling chickens.

"Oh, no. I'm not calling about the chickens," Indigo said.

"Ok?" More of a question than a statement.

Indigo cleared nir throat. It had taken a lot of preparation to figure out nir story. It had to be bombproof. No gaps for being turned down. Ne had to get down to the Eastern Cape and start investigating once ne got there.

"I'm calling from Centurion, here in Tshwane. I'm doing my matric at the moment, and we have to do some volunteer projects as part of the President's Award. I'm coming down to that part of the world and am really good with horses." *Well, at least that bit was true*, ne thought to nemself. Indigo had always been a passionate horse rider.

"I was hoping I could come and help out on your farm, even if it was just for a couple of days. I see you have Nooitgedachts...."

Indigo held nir breath. Once ne was there, ne would be able to steer the conversation towards the twins. Perhaps figure out where they lived or went to school....

"Oh," Nina said. "Well, that would be cool. I'm sure my grandmother would love that. But when are you coming? In a few days, we are going on holiday to a nature reserve near Sterkstroom."

Damn, Indigo thought. Patience was not nir strong suit.

"Well, actually, I was looking at flying down tomorrow. I know it is short notice."

There was a short pause on the other side. Indigo had the impression that Nina had put her hand over the speaker and was talking it over with someone. Then the girl came back online.

"Ok. I've got your number and will chat with my grandmother. We will need to figure out accommodation and all that."

A bossy voice suddenly cut in,

"And you need to send a CV. And a proposal. We will WhatsApp you an email address,"

Ok. So Nina had been on speakerphone all along.

"Who is that speaking?" Indigo asked politely.

"My name is Tess. I'm Nina's friend."

"And I'm Ryan," chimed in the high-pitched voice of a boy.

Indigo felt nir heart racing. On the table in front of nem was a printout of the photo of the six children in that article.

Tess! She was the twins' younger sister.

Bingo!

"Cool. Very nice to chat with you guys. I look forward to meeting all three of you."

Indigo put down the phone and, with near nausea, opened up the FlySafair website to look at available flight tickets to East London. Ne could rent a car on arrival and drive from there. Thank goodness ne had been organised enough to get nir driver's license as soon as ne had turned eighteen!

The wheels had been set in motion. Hopefully, Nina's grandmother would have no objections. It would be a bit of pain explaining to nir parents why ne was going off on such short notice, but the folks were getting used to nir unpredictable ways.

CHAPTER 6: *Arno*

It was just after dawn when Arno slid into the front passenger seat of the Black Mercedes and gave the chauffeur, Lerato Ngini, a wide grin. The elderly isiXhosa man exclaimed in horror, "*Hayi, buti.*[25] You must go and sit in the back. Mr Brandt won't like you sitting in the front like this."

The old man looked nervous as he parked outside one of the apartment blocks in Hanover Park. Being a chauffeur to one of the wealthiest men in Cape Town usually meant he never had to go anywhere near the flats. He stayed in a three-by-three metre room at the back of Mr Brandt's garage in the smart Clifton suburbs, available at the beck and call of his employer twenty-four hours a day.

"Ja, we mustn't tell the dear then, must we," Arno said, wiggling his eyebrows suggestively before he greeted the chauffeur. "*Kunjani*[26] *tata wam*[27]?"

Lerato rolled his eyes in exasperation, but Arno knew the chauffeur was a complete softy. And there was no way he, Arno Swart, was sitting

---

[25] No brother
[26] How is it
[27] My father.

in the back. Arno understood his place in the world, and it wasn't being driven around like a lord.

"*Hayi, sikhona*[28], Arno," Lerato replied as he started the car and quickly pulled out into the busy back roads of the Cape Flats.

"Hayi, Lerato. Why so fast, hey?" Arno laughed. "They won't steal the tires off your car while you're driving, bra."

"These *skollies*[29] might just try," Lerato grumbled under his breath but slowed down a bit before he added, "Mr Brandt wants us to leave by nine o'clock sharp, *buti*."

Arno scoffed, accentuating it with a graceful flick of his wrist, "No worries, Lerato. It is still blerrie early, my china."

They had a good hour's drive ahead with all the traffic, even though Hanover Park and Clifton both had a Cape Town postal code. Arno had hoped that Lerato would be the one to come and fetch him. The chauffeur might be able to explain to him what the hell was going on.

The youth fidgeted and wondered how to broach the subject. He dropped down the sun visor and quickly checked himself out in the mirror. He had toned it down today with just a little mascara and lip gloss today. He was growing out his curly, pitch-black hair, which was already just below his ears. It was neatly brushed back, set with just a bit of hair gel and tucked behind his ears. Jimmy hadn't seen it long like this yet, and Arno hadn't been posting any pics. Arno wondered whether his friend would like it. On second thoughts, Jimmy never noticed what Arno was wearing and probably wouldn't notice the new hairdo either.

Better to get this over with.

"Now, Lerato," Arno started as he popped back the visor and then paused to consider how to phrase his question. But he had never been one for subtleties.

"Andiyazi lo into[30]. We are going for a three-day visit to this game park, hey. And Mr Brandt is flying down to East London on Wednesday, right? So why on earth are Jimmy and I being driven the whole

---

[28] No, we (older isiXhosa people refer to themselves in this way) are well

[29] thieves

[30] I don't understand this thing

Superheroes in Sterkstroom

verdompte[31] 1 400 km, hey? Now tell me straight, Lerato. Is it me? Can Mr Brandt not handle the idea of a queer on the same aisle on the plane or what, bra?"

Arno kept his tone light. He was always the joker. That was the best way to get to the root of a thing.

But Arno had never gotten to the root of Marthinus Brandt.

A homophobic, chauvinistic, racist bastard as ever there was, yet the man had never interfered with Arno's friendship with his only son and heir. Even now. Take this fancy-pantsy business trip to the Eastern Cape. Arno got why Jimmy had invited him to come, Jimmy couldn't tie his own shoe laces without some backup, but why on earth did Mr Brandt agree?

Lerato shook his head mournfully, "You mustn't use that word, master Arno."

"Which one? *Verdompte?*" Arno cheeked the elderly man. Lerato just looked more upset.

Arno sighed, "No worries, Lerato. One is allowed to call oneself queer if you are one of the family, and I am Queer AF, honey."

Arno patted the chauffeur kindly on the shoulder. Even though the old man had never given Arno his full approval, the old man had always looked out for him.

Arno still remembered that time Jimmy had invited him home for the weekend. It was the first term of Grade 8, and they had been hanging out every break. The school had been very strict, and kids with sponsorships weren't allowed home from the hostel on weekends, only in the holidays. For Arno, those weekends at the hostel had been a dull, blank horror.

But then Jimmy and Arno had been tasked to build a rocket for their physics project, and Jimmy managed to convince his teachers, and his formidable father, that Arno needed to come home with him for the weekend to get the job done.

Lerato had picked them up at school that Friday afternoon. Jimmy and Arno had shuffled onto the back seat, high on excitement and

---

[31] damned

anticipation. Arno thought of himself as a bottle of Twizza, which, with a bit of shaking, can bubble over in a splendid fountain of joy.

And that day, he had been on full bubbles.

As they drove to Jimmy's house, Arno noticed Lerato watching him in the rearview mirror with a slight frown between his eyes. It challenged Arno to push his flamboyancy up another notch, secretly hoping to shock the elder into minding his own business.

He had never believed in hiding who he was. And to hell with the consequences.

They arrived at Jimmy's house, and for the first time in his life, Arno was speechless by the sheer splendour of it. He had known that Jimmy had to be rich - well, everyone at school was richer than he was. But he had only expected a nice house in a suburb, not a mansion on a cliff.

Lerato had eased the Mercedes up the steep driveway and parked in front of the huge marble arches that flanked the double oak door with their over-the-top big brass hinges. And then the old chauffeur Lerato had made use of Arno's temporary paralysis to say his piece. He had turned round and looked Arno straight in the eye,

"*Mamela, mntwana*[32]. I am not going to ask you to pretend to be what you are not. But you must know that you are everything that Mr Brandt despises." Jimmy tried to protest, but Lerato silenced him with a look and turned back to Arno. "But I will give you some advice. You are doing a school project this week, *kulungile*[33]?"

Arno had nodded mutely.

"You make sure that project gets a first in class. An A, nothing less. *Uyaqonda*? You go make yourself useful."

"But Lerato, *I* don't even get a C for Physics," Jimmy complained from the back seat, even though the comment was clearly not aimed at him.

"*Nyanisile*.[34]," Lerato said, still looking at Arno, but said no more.

Jimmy didn't get it, but Arno understood. If he could be a so-called 'good influence' on Mr Brandt's darling son, then maybe some other things could be overlooked.

---

[32] **Listen child**

[33] **Is it right?**

[34] **Exactly**

Superheroes in Sterkstroom

That first weekend at the Brandt's mansion wasn't easy, but Arno did not forget Lerato's words. And sure enough, Jimmy and Arno got an A for that project, and things were definitely easier after that. When they matriculated last year, Arno with an A for physics and Jimmy an unbelievable B, Marthinus Brandt had given them each a fancy watch and had seemed genuinely warm at their graduation.

And now this strange affront. Arno had worried about it since Jimmy had casually mentioned Mr Brandt's outrageous plan of getting his chauffeur to drive them down to the Eastern Cape instead of flying with the big boss himself. Perhaps it had to do with Arno being more obvious in his otherness now that he had left school. No more school uniforms to disguise his love for flamboyant, colourful scarves and skin-tight jeans.

Lerato interrupted his thoughts, "Now, what does queer AF mean, master Arno?"

Arno rolled his eyes, "Just queer and proud, Lerato. And stop calling me blerrie master. Now, what is the story, hey?"

Lerato pursed his lips, looking put out by the encounter. But he must have noticed Arno's agitation.

"No bhuti, *sukuzikathaza*.[35] This has nothing to do with you. Mr Brandt always does this."

Arno lifted an eyebrow, "Eh, what?"

Lerato smiled and added conspiratorially, "Mr Brandt doesn't like change. Likes things to be just so. Even sleeping in a strange bed unsettles him terribly. And getting a rental car, no ways could Mr Brandt stomach that. So whenever Mr Brandt has to travel, he likes to fly in and out, and if he has to stay for a few days, I must bring the car. He can't do without his car or his Lerato," the chauffeur added proudly.

Arno nodded in amazement. How had he never picked up this little bit of juicy rich-man gossip? Wait till he tells the *bras* back home. "And why are we driving with you and not flying with Mr Brandt?" Arno asked, still nervous about the answer.

---

[35] Don't worry yourself about it.

"That was master Jimmy's idea," Lerato said, "said he loves a road trip. He even organised the hotel in Knysna where you boys are staying over tonight."

Arno laughed. That he should have guessed, Jimmy would do anything to stay out of his father's way, even if it meant driving fourteen hours to avoid a one-hour flight.

"And where are you staying tonight, Lerato? Did Mr Brandt book you a nice room next door to ours?"

"Hayi, Arno, don't be disrespectful," Lerato said, but he was laughing. "I have a nice Airbnb not too far away. With good secure parking for the Merc."

Arno leaned back in his seat and breathed out slowly. A burden had lifted. There were no weird micro-aggressions going on here: just Mr Brandt and a bit of OCD.

And he and Jimmy were getting a few days on some exotic game reserve.

This was going to be blerrie legit.

CHAPTER 7: *Nina*

Nina gave Toast, her beautiful Palomino stallion, a good scratch behind the ears. The horse neighed happily, and Nina smiled. Although a part of her was looking forward to the trip to Mpangwa Nature Reserve, at heart, she was very much a homebody and was already worrying about leaving her horses, her chickens, and her dear mixed German Shephard/Labrador dog, Aero, behind. Mr Sibeko and Maria would ensure they were all fed and looked after, but no one understood her animals like she did. What if something went wrong? Who would they tell?

"Nina. They are here!" Nina could hear Ryan shouting from the other side of the field. He had been playing at the front gate all morning, waiting for Indigo to arrive, even though the flight was only scheduled to land in East London at 8.00 a.m., and it was a good two-hour drive.

Nina was confused. They? Did Indigo bring someone else as well?

Nina stepped outside the stable and watched as Ryan and Tess accompanied an impossibly tall person over the field. Nina realised she wasn't sure if it was a boy or a girl. She had made assumptions over the phone, but the name Indigo could obviously be either. Indigo had short, pitch-black hair with an angular face and a strong jaw. Although tall, the eighteen-year-old did not stoop but walked with strong, loping strides across the field. They were wearing ripped jeans and a black hoodie. Toast neighed softly.

"Ja, Toast. I know. That is our new groom for a couple of days."

Nina walked towards them, and Ryan rushed ahead to meet her.

"Nina, this is Indigo. And they are a *they*."

Ryan looked in his element, like he was the first human to make contact with a new exotic alien race that had just landed on Earth. Nina frowned in confusion.

"They are non-bilateral, you see. So they are neither male nor female. Isn't that just so cool?"

Indigo laughed, "The term is non-binary, Ryan. But you are forgiven for your flawless use of my pronoun."

Indigo's voice was rich and husky, and Nina realised that nothing about Indigo gave any clues about their so-called gender. They were truly neutral.

Tess glared at Ryan, "Geez, Ryan, don't make such a fuss. You will just embarrass them." And then turning to Indigo, "I'm afraid he doesn't get out much. In my school in East London, I have two kids in my class that are *trans*, but out here in the country, they still live in the Middle Ages."

Nina felt herself blushing. She was as much a country kid as Ryan was and had no idea about any of these things. Indigo was looking at her kindly.

"Don't worry, Nina. I'm not very fussed. I've lived as a non-binary for two years now. All you need to know is that I have some funny pronouns - instead of using he or she, you can use the plural them/ they. It's a bit confusing at first, but I won't get offended if you get it wrong. I just really appreciate it when people try."

Nina nodded and smiled. As she had no idea what gender Indigo might have been once upon a time, it did not seem too complicated to use the pronoun 'they' to refer to the beautiful tall youth.

The morning passed in a whirl as the three children introduced Indigo to the animals. The youth was fascinating and clearly competent in dealing with all the animals. Nina wondered if they might be willing to stay on and look after the animals whilst Nina was away. It would take some of the pressure off Mr Sibeko.

The children had just finished moving the two chicken tractors when Indigo turned to speak to Nina.

"I must confess that before I came, I Googled a bit about *Hog's Hollow*, and I came across an article about you guys saving some lives last year with your detective work. The article didn't give many details. I would love to hear the story."

Nina looked at Tess. This was definitely her arena, and Tess filled in happily.

"Ag, it wasn't much. Mr Sibeko, our groom here, was sick, and we realised he had been smoking some dodgy ciggies."

Tess said no more, and Nina hoped that Indigo would leave it at that, but Indigo seemed really interested.

They asked, "And the article said you have twin sisters, Tess. There was a photo. They look really cool."

"Very cool," Tess agreed.

"Awesome!" Ryan added.

"Yes, they are very nice," Nina said, trying to think of a way to change the topic.

Indigo seemed a bit nonplussed but pushed on. "Where are your sisters now, Tess? And that hero, Dawie Stuurman?"

"Oh, the twins are at home in East London. They are also in matric and because of everything they have to study. Anyway, they would just think it is boring here. And Dawie is at university at NMU studying graphic design. He and Bonnie is a thing…"

Nina watched Indigo closely. They were following Tess' words with great interest. And although Nina was better at understanding animals than people, she could see that Indigo knew there was more to the story, but they didn't say anything else.

Just then, Alex's *bakkie* came to a screeching halt in the Hog's Hollow driveway.

"Who is that?" Indigo asked.

"The vet," Tess answered, but Nina was already running towards the vehicle as she heard Tess explain, "Something is wrong. She must be here for Nina."

Madeleine Muller

Alex opened the driver's door and gave Nina a strained smile,

"Oh, thank goodness you are here. I need your help. I have an injured dog in the back. It looks like it was either hit by a car or maybe even in a car that was involved in an accident. It came limping out of the forest not far from here. It is completely frantic, and I think it is trying to tell us something."

Nina nodded and accompanied Alex to the back of the double cab. The inside was cleverly set up with padded cages and an area for examination and minor emergency procedures. It was like a mobile clinic for small animals. In one cage was a small, adorable sausage dog. It had streaks of blood on its back legs, and it was limping round and round in circles, clearly in distress.

"I haven't given it anything for the pain yet," Alex said. "I didn't want to sedate it until we knew what was going on. I need to set that leg, though."

Nina nodded and started to open the cage.

"Careful," she heard Alex say, but she was already entering that quiet place, focusing only on the dog. It stopped circling and looked at her, and when she put out her arms, it limped to her without hesitating. It was a large cage that could easily house a Great Dane, so Nina sat down in its small, confined space and carefully placed the dog on her lap. She stroked it and felt herself pulled into a vortex of pain and panic.

A year or so ago, Nina would have been lost in the animal's distress, but she had been practising and found it easy to keep a part of her separate. This was her 'balcony view.' A place where part of her could look out at everything she was feeling and yet not be right in it. It helped her to understand what was going on, to gain perspective.

In the chaos of the dog's fear, images started to arise. Although the images were disjointed and chaotic, Nina could quickly put it all together.

"There was a car accident. And the dog was in the car," she said. "Two people in the front, the dog in the back seat. The car rolled, and the dog was thrown out of the car. I think the car rolled down a steep incline and is quite far down from the road. The dog couldn't reach the car, so I am not sure if the people inside are ok. I think they are quite old. The poor thing limped through the forest to try and get help."

Superheroes in Sterkstroom

Alex nodded, "Any clues as to where it happened?"

"Do you know where the dog came out of the forest?" Nina asked in return. "I think it pretty much ran in a straight line through the bush - it wasn't following any road or paths."

"Yes, I do," Alex said. "The people who found it said they picked it up at that massive oak near *Hala*."

"Good work," Tess said, and Nina suddenly became aware of her surroundings - Alex was sitting next to her in the back of the *bakkie*; Tess was already searching Google Earth on her iPad with Ryan tripping from foot to foot in barely held excitement and Indigo watching her with quiet concentration. Nina blushed in mortification. She had completely forgotten about Indigo. Alex looked puzzled for a moment, and then she also registered the newcomer.

"Oh. Hi," she said. "Who is this?"

Indigo put our their hand, "Hi, my name is Indigo. I am a volunteer here on the farm. I hope I can be of assistance."

Alex shook their hand and seemed unsure of how to explain what was going on.

But as usual, Tess just took charge.

"Ok. If you start from Hala and take a straight line up through the forest, you get to the R345 on the Hogsback pass. They probably rolled off that steep cliff there somewhere."

"Right," Alex sighed. "This is terrible. Let me just call the police and let them know. I need to get this one back to the surgery to set its leg. Well done, Nina. Not such a nice case this."

CHAPTER 8: *Indigo*

Indigo carefully manoeuvred the little rental car around the hair pin bends of the R345. After Alex had left, Indigo had managed to convince the three kids to go and see if they could help locate the accident site whilst waiting for the police to arrive. It was impossible to tell if the old couple, if Nina had guessed that correctly, may have been found already, but if they hadn't, Nina was worried about the severely understaffed local police station and that the only police car may be more than an hour away.

Indigo understood that there was no quicker way to gain the children's trust than to become an accomplice in their adventure.

Ne had been looking for the twins, but it was clear that Nina had a whole set of gifts of her own. Indigo didn't ask, but it didn't take much to see that Nina had been able to get into the head of that little dog, see what the poor thing had seen and figure out what had happened. And Alex, the vet, clearly trusted her skills, which was why she came to ask for her help.

Indigo wondered about Tess and Ryan.

Tess was clearly the organised one and did all the bossing around, but that was not really a superpower. And Ryan. Ne had a hunch that if

Superheroes in Sterkstroom

Ryan had a superpower, they would know what it was by now. He did not seem the kind of kid who could keep a secret....

"Ok, you better slow down; this is the start of the Hogsback pass," Tess said. "It will be somewhere over the next couple of kilometres."

Indigo slowed down and fought the temptation to help scour the roadside. The road was very narrow, snaking up the side of a mountain covered in thick, impenetrable indigenous forest. Although ne had passed nir driver's license with flying colours, ne was aware of the responsibility of the three children in nir car.

On their left, the road hugged the steep cliff, while on the right, the forest dropped down steeply into the valley below. Indigo felt nir heart rate increase. What if ne couldn't find the crashed car? This was a wild, isolated place

.

But it turned out to be pretty easy after all. After only a couple of steep turns, Ryan called out.

"There!"

Indigo slowed down and found a place to safely park the car. If you looked for it, the tyre marks on the road were easy to see, leading right towards the edge, the bushes clearly flattened. But there was no sign of the vehicle, and a casual passerby might easily miss it.

"I think you kids better wait here," Indigo instructed. "This might be messy."

"Hey, who are you calling kids!" Ryan snorted. "We ain't kids; we are the K.I.D. And this is our turf."

Ryan folded his arms and lifted his eyebrows, and Nina giggled. Tess simply pushed past Indigo towards the edge and carefully peered over the side.

"I can see it. A white car. Lying on its side. Only the wheels are visible from here. It's quite a bit down, but it's not too steep. We should be able to get to it with a bit of scrambling. I will forward a location to Alex to send to the police and the ambulance. Ryan, get the first aid kit."

Ryan gave Indigo a "told you so" look and went to grab a massive green Dischem first aid backpack out of the car.

Indigo tried to suppress a smile.

Madeleine Muller

Since ne discovered nir powers, ne had always considered it nir responsibility, and also nir privilege, to get involved in any crisis that needed solving. A bit of a *'friendly local Spiderman'* complex going on - and clearly, these three kids had the exact same attitude.

Scrambling was certainly a good prediction of what it would take to reach the car, and all four of them were covered in mud and grime by the time they reached the overturned vehicle. It had been raining the night before, and with the high trees and thick undergrowth, everything was still soaked. It was probably the wet road that had contributed to the car going over that edge.

As they approached the car, Indigo's apprehension grew. It was lying on its side with the tyres facing them. Tess had done various calculations whilst they had been driving here, based on the time it would have taken the dog to limp across the forest, then to be found and brought to Hog's Hollow. Taking all that into account, the accident must have happened at least three hours ago - possibly much longer.

Indigo assumed the worst.

But as they neared the car, they could hear a noise. At first, Indigo thought that maybe it was someone groaning, but then ne realised it was soft sobbing.

"Hello," Indigo called out, not wanting to frighten the occupants. Ne noticed the three children hesitating, the reality hitting home.

A frail woman's voice answered back, "Hello, *Bitte helfen. Wie ist dar?*" She sounded distressed and distraught and was speaking in what sounded like German.

"Don't worry. We have found you," Indigo said as ne made nir way to the car. "We have called the police and the ambulance."

The car had made an indentation in the thick bush, and Indigo had to carefully push branches away to get to the other side of the vehicle. The front window had cracks running all over it but wasn't shattered. In the driver's seat, closest to the ground, was a middle-aged man with brown hair peppered with grey, still strapped in. His eyes were closed, and he wasn't moving. He had a nasty cut of dried blood on his forehead. Indigo hoped he was only unconscious. A much older lady, Indigo assumed his mother, must have unclipped herself with great difficulty from the passenger seat and had climbed into the back of the car. Indigo guessed that she had been unable to get herself out. Her grey hair was matted with blood, and she was peering out over the back seat, trying to locate Indigo.

"Hi," Indigo shouted, "I am over here."

"Bitte! Helfen," the lady shouted again, still trying to peer through the cracked windscreen, and Indigo guessed that the old woman could not see very well. And she was speaking German.

"Can you speak English?" Indigo shouted.

"Helfen! Helfen!" was the only reply, her voice weak and trembling. Indigo guessed the old lady was exhausted and in complete panic.

"Know any German?" Ryan's voice popped up at Indigo's elbow and gave nem a fright. "I can speak to her in Afrikaans. Do you think that will work?"

Indigo shook nir head, suddenly not sure what to say. Ne didn't speak German, but there were ways and means… If the kids hadn't been here….

Tess was gingerly beating down the bush on the left-hand side of the car, trying to get closer to the windscreen.

"She must be German. Nina, you ever learnt any German back in Joburg?" But Tess didn't wait for an answer and was now softly knocking on the front screen.

"Hello, Auntie. We are going to help you. Can you speak English?"

The old lady gave a start, but as she spotted Tess, she started wailing hysterically. Tess got such a fright she took a step back. The old lady was trying to climb into the front of the car, towards Tess' voice, and the car was rocking dangerously.

"Stop! Stop!" Tess shouted in alarm, and for a moment, the woman paused, tears streaming down her cheeks.

Indigo made a decision. Sometimes you can't overthink these things too much. Ne needed to speak to the old woman. Ne turned to Nina.

"Nina, I've noted you have a certain talent for talking to animals." Nina looked at her intently but did not answer. Indigo continued, "Well, I have a little talent of my own."

Madeleine Muller

"No way!" Ryan exclaimed, his eyes wide and his voice a husky whisper.

"Tess, can I quickly borrow your iPad? You seem to have some reception here."

Tess handed it to Indigo without a quibble, and ne quickly looked up a German news agency whilst trying to explain nir bizarre talent to these three unlikely accomplices.

"I am able to shapeshift into a different shape when I need to. Not completely someone else's body, but a version of them. And I can gain that person's skills – like, for example, the language they speak."

"Like Mystique…" Ryan's voice was still just above a whisper in reverent awe

Indigo smiled, "Not exactly. I still look a bit like myself, or so I was once told. For some reason, I can't see the shape I shift into. And to be honest, I have not had a lot of, well, witnesses to this little trick of mine."

"Awesome," Ryan whispered.

Even Tess had lost her usual calm when she answered, "Ok. Wow. So you are going to become some German person now?"

The old lady was still sobbing softly in the background.

Indigo nodded as ne played a short clip from a German news reporter.

"Yip, but I need some point of reference. Like this news reporter."

Ne looked up at the kids. This would be the first time ne had shifted with anyone else actually watching; ne could feel nir heart starting to race.

"Ready?" ne asked, wondering if this was such a good idea. The kids nodded expectantly, and Indigo suddenly felt a small twinge of elation. This was what it was like when you found your own kind.

Ne closed nir eyes and felt that slight vertigo as ne shifted.

"*Blerrie hel!*" Ryan exclaimed, "that is full-on legit."

Indigo opened nir eyes and looked nervously at the three kids. Ryan was smiling, clearly over the moon. Nina gave nem a supportive pat on the shoulder as if she knew what it was to first reveal your power, and Tess simply gave nem a professional nod.

"That is a cool look. So you can speak German now?"

Superheroes in Sterkstroom

Indigo realised that, for a moment, ne had completely forgotten about why ne had shifted in the first place. Ne squeezed past Tess and pressed nir face as close to the windscreen as ne dared.

In Indigo's head, ne were still speaking English, but there was a strange feel to the air around nir voice box, to the way the words tasted and ne knew from past experience that what was coming out would be fluent German.

"Mam, can you hear me? My name is Indigo. I need you to take a deep breath."

The old lady had retreated onto the back seat again but now leaned forward.

"Hello? You speak German? Oh, thank God. I am visiting my son from Germany, and my English is very poor. We have been in a terrible accident. Oh, please, can you help us?"

"The police and the ambulance are on their way," Indigo soothed her before they asked, "Are you hurt?"

"No, I am ok," and then the woman started crying again softly. "But my son. I don't know. He was awake at first but very confused, but now he is all quiet. I am frightened to move in the car to check him."

"Here is a torch," Tess said as she handed Indigo a head torch out of her bag. Indigo shone the light through the windscreen onto the man's chest. He looked like a child, curled up on his side to sleep. With relief, ne noticed his chest moving.

"Mam, your son is still breathing. He is just unconscious. What is your name?"

"Ida. I'm Ida Kohler."

"Hi, Frau Kohler. Just sit tight. Are you thirsty?"

The old lady nodded mutely, and Indigo turned back to the other three, "Ryan, you look pretty nimble. That passenger window is half open. I'll lift you up, and you can pass some water to Frau Kohler."

"And I've got some energy bars," Tess said.

As Tess scrounged through her bag to get out the necessary supplies, Indigo turned to Nina.

"Can I ask you something? Can you tell me what I look like?"

"I can take a picture if you like?" Nina offered.

Madeleine Muller

Indigo shook nir head, "It will just be me in the pic. It is like the shape is some sort of illusion. I can't pick it up in a mirror or on a camera. I've tried before."

Nina didn't ask any more questions but took a small step back. "Well, you are male - still the same height, and your hair is the same pitch-black colour, but it is longer. And your face is broader and more masculine, but it is still your hazel-coloured eyes. And your clothes are different. You are wearing a suit. It's like an older, German version of you."

Indigo sighed a deep sigh of completion. For years now, ne has been alone, so terribly alone.

But not today. In this small, rural village in the Eastern Cape, ne had found nir people. They were certainly not quite the glamorous superheroes ne had always imagined; as a matter of fact, it felt more like family. Better in some ways.

"Okey, dokey. Mission Impossible, ready for action," Ryan chimed in. He had a plastic Checkers bag with water, food, gauze and tissues ready in one hand. "Let's do this."

"I'm not sure this will fly under the MI franchise," Indigo said drily but smiled as ne carefully lifted Ryan towards the top of the car, who then deftly lowered the supplies to Frau Kohler.

A family with two younger sisters and a pesky younger brother. Absolutely perfect.

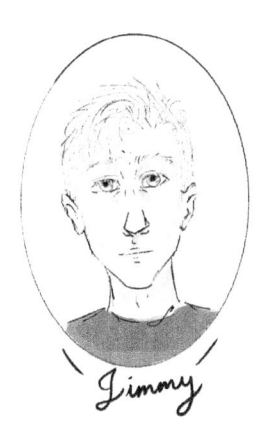

CHAPTER 9: *Jimmy*

Jimmy watched as Arno put in the last few stitches. His friend was bent over the suit trousers in quiet concentration, and Jimmy already knew that the work would be flawless. They were sitting in their bungalow at Mpangwa Reserve and had an hour before they were expected for supper at the main restaurant.

Even after two days on the road together, Jimmy was still getting used to Arno's new look. His curly black hair was hooked behind his ears, almost a 1920's style, with strands of escaped locks hanging over his face. Jimmy noted a new ear piercing, and Jimmy quietly counted a variety of six earrings in his left ear. Arno's eyes flicked up, and Jimmy looked away. Arno looked great. Like someone out of a movie.

"Almost done, lovey. You just need to find us an iron, and you will be the proud owner of the perfect Brad Pitt suit!"

*

They had been just about to leave Cape Town, with Lerato loading the bags in the boot of the Mercedes, when Mr Brandt had stepped out to say goodbye. Not usually a sentimental man, Jimmy had suspected something was afoot and felt his heart drop when his father had walked over to Arno.

"Arno, son. I have a job for you."

Madeleine Muller

Jimmy was sure Arno must have been having a small panic attack, but his friend simply lifted an eyebrow.

"Sure, Mr Brandt. What's up?"

Mr Brandt smiled. Jimmy suspected that it amused him that Arno did not seem cowed by him like the rest of the world.

"This ragamuffin son of mine is stepping into the world now. I expect him to make an impression at our meeting at Mpangwa, and he is not going to do it looking like that. You understand style, don't you, Arno?" The way Marthinus Brandt used the word *style*, you could feel the gold dripping off it.

"You mean like the '*I might be young, but I am the future of this corporation*' style, Mr Brandt? Classy, but modern? Well-fitted and easily worn?"

Mr Brandt laughed, "Exactly. I thought you were the man, or, whatever you are, for the job. Jimmy needs the right suit. There are a couple of excellent tailors with a wide range of suits in Knysna. Lerato knows them well and will take you there. I've given Jimmy my credit card. I am putting you in charge of his wardrobe, as they say. Hopefully, you can find something that will fit in such a short time."

"No worries, Mr Brandt," Arno effused excitedly, clasping his hands together. Jimmy inwardly rolled his eyes. "We will get him suited up. And I can do any alterations on the road, no worries. Any colour preferences?"

Mr Brandt shook his head, now looking straight at Jimmy.

"I'll leave that up to you, Arno - think corporate and successful. And no pink."

"Really?" Arno pouted. "Pity."

Mr Brandt shot him a quick glare, and Arno gave his best 'just joking' lifted eyebrow smile, but Jimmy could see his dad wasn't worried. Mr Brandt had more faith in Arno than his own son. Sometimes Jimmy wasn't sure if this was a good or a bad thing.

They had found a well-cut dark turquoise suit with crisp white shirts and a range of beautiful ties to go with it. Jimmy had been grumpy throughout the whole shopping expedition, desperate to go boating on the Knysna lagoon, but Arno had been in his element. Fashion was his craft, and dressing his best friend on a credit card with no limit… surely there was nothing better than that.

*

The dinner that evening at the Mpangwa dining room was supposed to be an informal affair, but Mr Brandt had sent Jimmy a detailed email of what was expected. They would be meeting with the Mpangwa management and the National Parks Board. The real negotiations would only begin the following day, but tonight was all about making impressions. "Trust," Mr Brandt had emphasised. "By the end of tonight, it must feel like family."

Arno looked up at Jimmy again and this time raised his voice a notch. "We need a *Strykyster*[36], darling. Whatever are you thinking? Go ask at reception. I'm sure that nice girl, Susan, will be able to help."

The heart of the Mpangwa Reserve Lodge was a large, thatched roof building with a huge tiled entrance area and counters made of thick, darkly varnished rough-cut timber. On the left, the reception led to the restaurant, and on the other side, to a boardroom and conference area, with various rooms for 'breakaway' sessions. Surrounding this central building were various thatched bungalows, cool and spacious, which made up the accommodation. It was supposed to be that particular version of 'smart' rustic, but even Jimmy's untrained eye could see that things were fraying at the edges. The grass was growing through the paving and creeping over the neat beds of aloes laid out around the buildings; the wooden countertops needed to be resanded, and there was mould on the grout between the floor tiles.

He found Susan, a friendly plump girl about his age, the only person behind the counter at the Mpangwa Lodge reception.

"You need some help with the ironing? I can ask one of our ladies?" Susan asked in a heavy Afrikaans accent as she placed the iron on the counter.

"*Nee, dankie.*[37]" Jimmy said in his best school Afrikaans. "My friend can do it."

---

[36] iron

[37] No, thank you

"Is he your boyfriend?" Susan asked, clearly curious. Jimmy was so surprised by the question that he found himself fumbling.

"What? No, hey. Nee. We are just friends, like."

Susan's smile widened even more, but before she could say anything else, Jimmy grabbed the iron off the counter and headed out the large glass sliding doors. As he turned the corner, he ran straight into a wall. Or at least it felt like a wall.

"*Heibo*! Watch out!"

Jimmy looked up into the handsome face of the largest black man he had ever seen. He was several heads higher than Jimmy, with a shaven head and a thick, bushy beard. Jimmy noted the khaki uniform with green epaulettes on the shoulders and swallowed nervously. Some sort of soldier?

"Sorry, Sir," he fumbled and wondered if there would ever be a time in his life when he wouldn't be on the back foot.

"*Molo, mtwana*[38]," the big black man said. "*Unjani*[39]?"

"*Hayi, sikhona mhlekaz'. Unjani wena?*[40]" Jimmy was suddenly grateful at Lerato always insisting that they practice the isiXhosa greeting, the mother tongue of the Eastern Cape. The black man nodded his approval, smiled, and put out his hand.

"I am Abongile. It is very nice to meet you."

Jimmy's hand was engulfed in the black man's hand. Abongile put his left hand on Jimmy's wrist, isiXhosa style, making him feel even smaller.

"And I am Jimmy. I mean James. I am James Brandt," Jimmy managed to squeak out, his voice sounding much too young in his ears.

Abongile gave a little frown, "Brandt? You are the son of Marthinus Brandt?"

Jimmy nodded enthusiastically, "Yes. That's right."

"On holiday," Abongile said. More a statement than a question, and Jimmy blushed. The man thought him a child.

"No," he protested weakly. "I work at the Brandt Corporation. I am part of the negotiating team."

---

[38] Hello, child

[39] How are you

[40] No, we are fine Sir, And you how are you?

Superheroes in Sterkstroom

Abongile's eyes narrowed slightly, but then he smiled.

"I see. Impressive. It sounds like a difficult job. What are you hoping to achieve in tomorrow's meeting, then?"

Jimmy cleared his throat and tried to deepen his voice slightly, practising his elevator pitch as his father had instructed.

"Well, you see, we believe we can bring prosperity and a new lease of life to this part of the world. The nature reserve is clearly on its last legs...."

"James!" Mr Brandt's voice echoed over the parking lot. Jimmy involuntarily jumped at his father's voice and felt himself wince. He could feel Abongile's eyes watching him.

"Oh, hi, Dad. I mean, Mr Brandt."

Jimmy couldn't get used to calling his father by his title in formal situations. "This is...."

"Get away from there," Mr Brandt instructed, visibly seething. Jimmy was shocked by his father's rudeness and nervously looked at Abongile. The black man's face was a careful blank, his lips squeezed into a narrow line. Mr Brandt was a huge man himself, but even he only reached the height of Abongile's nose.

"What are you doing here?" Marthinus Brandt shouted at Abongile, "I told you, and I told your boss. The Green Scorpions have no business here. This is a private game reserve. You hear?"

Abongile turned to face Mr Brandt head-on and folded his large, muscular arms over his chest. Mr Brandt was all girth, soft and pudgy, whereas Abongile was solid muscle. Secretly Jimmy delighted in seeing his father outgunned in size for a change - the powerful black man towering over the soft corporate white CEO.

"And as I have said, Mr Brandt, the Green Scorpions look after all fauna and flora. The private industry does not own nature."

"It does here," Mr Brandt bristled, but he was clearly unsettled by Abongile's size and said no more. He grabbed Jimmy by the arm and dragged him away without a backward glance. Jimmy felt like protesting, sure his father's pinch-like grasp would leave bruises, but he didn't want to seem like a wimp in front of the ranger.

Madeleine Muller

When they were out of earshot, Mr Brandt said, "You stay away from that man, you hear me. And keep your mouth shut," before pushing him in the direction of his bungalow. "Now get dressed. Dinner is at 7.00 p.m."

Jimmy ran-stumbled to their one-roomed cottage, burst through the door and slammed it shut behind him. The whole incident caught up with him, and he could feel his heart racing. He struggled to catch his breath, and his legs felt like they could no longer carry him. He was still clutching the iron to his chest.

Arno was at his side in a flash, "Jimmy! *Hey, skattie. Wat nou*[41]?"

Jimmy looked at the concern in his friend's eyes and felt tears welling up.

"Panic attack?" Arno checked, and Jimmy nodded, suddenly enormously grateful that he had Arno at his side.

"Ok. Deep breath, remem'er. And do that exercise - the one you tol' me about? Five-four-three-two-one, hey? Tell me the steps again." As Arno spoke, he led Jimmy to one of the single beds and helped him sit down.

Jimmy answered, focusing only on the voice of his friend.

"Find five things you can see, four things you can hear, three things you can touch, two things you can smell, one thing you can taste."

"Off you go then," Arno said, pouring Jimmy a glass of water out of a jug covered by a beaded lace doily. Step by step, Jimmy did the exercise his therapist had taught him. It was a simple mindfulness trick - focusing so hard on finding things in the present that it helped to quiet all the unhelpful thoughts that were driving the anxiety - panicking about panicking.

Jimmy noted the off-brown colour of the round walls, the smooth varnish of the yellowwood set of drawers, the large, iron-wrought light fitting, and the black plastic kettle with two mugs on a melanin tray with elephant prints on it. By the time he picked out the high-pitched sounds of the cicadas outside and the lazy sound of the fan, he could already feel his heart calming down. As he reached the last step - one thing he could

---

[41] Hey, treasure. What is happening?

taste - Arno passed him the ball of Lindor chocolate that they had found on arrival, placed on freshly folded towels. Jimmy smiled as he popped it into his mouth. Although his panic attacks had not reduced in intensity over time, he was getting much better at getting out of them.

Arno sat patiently next to him on the single bed, still holding the glass of water and looking at him intently.

"Ok, so what's happening, darling? And don't just say your dad. Come on. Spill."

Jimmy considered for a moment. But he had to talk to someone. And here was his friend, the only person in the world he could trust.

"It's this deal my dad is making. I don't like it. I… I don't want to be here."

Arno sighed, "Jimmy, sweetheart. We've been through this before. You gotta see the silver lining here, babe. I know this place is a bit of a wreck, but your dad buying a game farm is the best blerrie thing ever. And now that we are here, I am even more sure. All this place needs is a bit of a makeover, and am I not the 'Fab. Five' all in one? And did you see the art here - so gaudy. You are way better. Remember when we were in Grade 11, and you said all you wanted to do was paint? We can convince your dad to commission you for all the paintings."

As Arno spoke, Jimmy was shaking his head in quiet protest, "You don't understand, Arno. He isn't buying the damn nature reserve to try and revamp it or anything. I also thought so at first, but we had this meeting with Shoal Oil last week. I think my dad is brokering some deal…."

Arno's eyes widened in shock, "Shoal Oil? Hey? No way. Aren't they the guys trying to frack parts of the Northern Karoo?"

Jimmy nodded mutely.

"Your dad wants to sell the nature reserve for fracking? But surely that would never be allowed?"

"I don't know," Jimmy sniffed. "It's all very hush-hush, and my dad has not explained anything. I don't know any of the details. And remember I told you about Dr Kuzmich?"

"That creepy guy at the meeting? With the sweaty armpits?"

Madeleine Muller

Jimmy gave a small smile. Trust Arno to remember the armpits. Marthinus Brandt and Dr Kuzmich went back many years. He was a so-called business associate, but Jimmy had never liked the small, stringy man with his greasy hair and shiny complexion. He was always sweating, with dark stains under his armpits and down the back of his short-sleeved buttoned-down brown shirts.

"My dad has known him for years. He moved down to the Eastern Cape almost ten years ago but now has some position on the National Parks board."

"Not a medical doctor, then?" Arno asked.

"No. He has some conservancy degree. Although he does not seem particularly concerned about the environment. It was he who contacted my dad and told him about Mpangwa. I don't know what their scheme is, but I know it involves big money."

Arno thought it over.

"So what's supposed to happen at this fancy-pantsy meeting then?"

Jimmy felt nervous as he continued. Arno was not going to like this, "Well, the Mpangwa Nature Reserve is owned by this old lady, Mrs Alice Braithwaite. It has been in her family for, like, forever. She is running it as a cooperative with the local community, and most of the day-to-day running is done by the manager, Mr Mzi Dyani. So they share the profits, and at the moment, all of it will go to the cooperative when she dies. My dad wants to buy the lodge but can only do so with her approval. The whole point of this expedition is to convince her to sell...."

Arno folded his arms over his chest, clearly annoyed.

"*Liewe Hemel,*[42] Jimmy. We have been on the road for two days, and not a word of this. Your father is like the crook in every blerrie eco-warrior movie, and you are just going along with it?"

Jimmy's heart sank, and his voice dropped to a whisper, "Please, Arno. I am not supposed to say anything to anybody, and my dad specifically told me not to tell you anything. If old Mrs Braithwaite gets any wind of the real reason my dad is bidding for the nature reserve...."

---

[42] Dear Heaven

Superheroes in Sterkstroom

Arno scoffed, "This is dirty politics of the worst degree, Jimmy. How can you be a part of this? Last year we were part of the protests against Shell fracking the Wild Coast, and now you are the one paving the way to destroy this beautiful place."

Jimmy shook his head angrily, "It's not like that. This place is gone anyway. The animals are dying and migrating, and the lodge is basically bankrupt. It's not some pristine piece of landscape or anything."

But Arno would have none of it. They argued angrily for another hour till Jimmy pleaded desperately.

"Please, Arno. Please don't say anything. Let us just see what happens first. The Green Scorpions are here- maybe they will sort it all out, and nothing will happen anyway."

"Green Scorpions?" Arno asked.

"They are like a part of the police force that does environmental crimes, like hunting poachers and things," Jimmy explained. "I ran into one of their rangers when I fetched the iron, and my dad almost completely lost it when he saw me speaking to him. That's why I got the panic attack."

And with that, Jimmy felt the tears welling up again. He didn't want this. Not any of it.

Arno sighed and put his arm around his friend's shoulders.

"No worries, *skattie*. I won't say anything. But that doesn't mean I cannot snoop around a bit, hey? Green Scorpions *nogal*? I've always liked a man in uniform."

Jimmy smiled through the tears as he punched Arno on the shoulder, "*Hiert* Arno. No man. Abongile is huge. And terrifying. And anyway, he is old. Just be discreet, ok?"

"Honey…" Arno said, putting his hand on his chest, "I am the queen of discretion."

Madeleine Muller

CHAPTER 10: *Tess*

Ryan was about to get out of the bakkie to open the Mpangwa gate when the large metal contraption opened effortlessly on its own.

"It's electric, Ryan," Tess chirped next to him in the backseat of Alex's vehicle, and Ryan stuck out his tongue at her. The gate was an impressive affair with a guardhouse on each side (currently deserted) and covered with a large rectangular thatch roof. Tess looked with interest at the *Mpangwa Nature Reserve* sign - the paint was peeling, and the lettering faded. The place looked deserted.

"Are you sure that they are still open for business, Alex? Maybe they are closed after the whole COVID fiasco?" Tess asked as Alex drove the bakkie over the cattle grid that lay under the gate. On each side, a tall game fence stretched in either direction. The gate closed promptly behind them, and Alex slowed to read a small sign pointing to the road to take to the reception. She looked in the rearview mirror at Tess as she replied,

"Don't worry, Tess. Abongile has booked us a couple of bungalows. The lodge is still open, but I think they are struggling financially. They are only too happy for the customers. Abongile told Mr Dyani that you guys are doing a Green Scorpion elective and that I am a vet assisting the programme.

Superheroes in Sterkstroom

"Well, he wasn't lying," Ryan giggled from the back seat. "The Green Scorpions have got K.I.D on their payroll."

"They are not paying us, Ryan," Nina retorted irritably from the front seat.

"Ja, hey. Then who is paying for our *slaap-plek*[13]?"

Tess couldn't argue with that. When Alex had discussed the trip with their respective parents, she had mentioned that all the expenses would be covered. It was a pretty good deal for a place like this, run-down or not.

Alex pulled up her double cab bakkie in front of a large thatched building. Dotted behind and around it were sets of rondawels and bungalows - Tess assumed this was the accommodation for tourists and travellers coming to 'experience a bit of nature.'

"Nina, are you ok?" Alex asked, and Tess got a fright when she looked at her friend. Nina was lying curled up against the door in the front seat, her eyes closed. She opened them as Alex touched her gently on the shoulder.

"I'm fine. I'm just not feeling well. I think maybe I'm a bit car sick. I feel very heavy and tired."

"Well, you wait in the car, and we will go in and get our room key. Looks like you need a little lie-down." Alex patted Nina on the shoulder.

"Would you like me to wait with you in the car, Nina?" Tess asked although she was dying to start looking around. Ryan had already jumped out and was wandering around inspecting all and sundry.

"No, don't worry," Nina replied. "I'm sure I'll be fine in a minute."

Tess and Ryan accompanied Alex into the building and approached the long, veneered wooden counter. Behind it was a girl with her blonde-brown hair tied up in a pony, dressed in khaki shorts, matching t-shirt and a khaki sleeveless padded jacket. She smiled a bright, bubbly smile as they approached.

Excellent, Tess thought, *a friendly and hopefully chatty receptionist.*

---

[13] accommodation

Madeleine Muller

"Good afternoon, and welcome to Mpangwa Nature Reserve," the girl chirped in a high-pitched voice. "My name is Susan. Are you booking in?" Tess guessed the girl wasn't even twenty-years-old.

"Good afternoon," Alex replied, "Yes, please. Abongile made the booking. Dr Alex Summers."

"Cool," said Susan. "Are you like a doctor?"

"Vet," was all Alex said, and Tess rolled her eyes inwardly. Thank goodness they were here. Alex did not know the first thing about information gathering. It was all about chatting. But Susan was not deterred.

"Really? A vet. Oh, that is so great. I wonder if you would be able to look at Nyama, maybe. We have all been so worried. Mrs Braithwaite called the vet in Queenstown, but he is only able to come out next week."

"Nyama?" Tess prompted.

"He is our pet cheetah. Mrs Braithwaite took him in when he was orphaned ten years ago, and he was basically raised as the house cat. Or maybe like a dog. I don't know. But he is not well. He is not eating and has lost so much weight. Mzi cooks him steak every night, but he just sniffs at the stuff like it's dog pellets or something."

Tess gave Alex a pointed look. This was the perfect opportunity to inspect one of these sick animals first-hand, but Alex did not need any encouragement, "Ah, yes. I think Abongile may have mentioned an ill animal. I would be very happy to have a look. Maybe tomorrow morning before breakfast?"

"Cool," Susan replied enthusiastically, "That would be so awesome. I will tell Mzi; he is Mr Dyani, our manager here, and he adores Nyama. You are all booked into the family bungalow, number 4 *Warthog* cottage. It has three rooms, with its own kitchen and bathroom, and I see you have been booked for full board."

Ryan gave Tess a quizzical look, and she whispered an explanation, "It means all meals included,"

"Bonus!" Ryan whispered back.

Susan continued, "Supper is at 7.00 p.m. tonight. Do you need an iron? I can bring it around later. Someone has just borrowed it."

"An iron what?" Ryan asked, looking clearly puzzled.

Superheroes in Sterkstroom

Tess did not even disguise her exasperation, " Oh, for goodness sake Ryan. An iron - for ironing clothes…."

Ryan frowned, "*Wie op aarde*[44] would want to iron their clothes on holiday?"

Susan leaned forward over the counter and exclaimed proudly, "Not everyone comes here just for a holiday. Mpangwa Nature Reserve is also a conference centre. We have some very important people here this week. For business meetings and such like."

Tess wanted to ask more, but Alex interrupted her.

"Come on, kids. Let's get going. I want to get Nina out of that car. She was not looking well. Abongile is meeting us for supper tonight, and we need to unpack."

As Alex left, Tess went up to the counter, "It was nice meeting you, Susan. And I am super interested to hear about your work at a nature reserve. It sounds really awesome, with pet cheetahs and all that."

Susan beamed back in response, "Ja, sure, hey. Pop in anytime, and I will show you around."

Tess followed Alex and Ryan, her eyes scanning the reception. What would a lot of important people be doing in a dump like this? And the pet cheetah is also sick. So it was not just the wild animals in the park that had been affected.

Something wasn't right, and she was itching to find out what.

---

[44] Who on Earth

Madeleine Muller

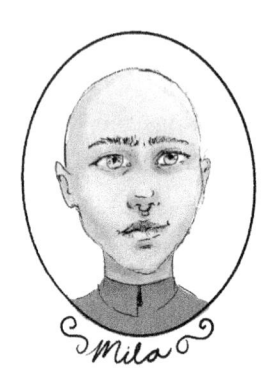

Chapter 11: *Bonnie & Mila*

    Bonnie and Mila paddled lazily over the swell and found a spot to wait for a good set to come through. They had spent the whole morning working through some past matric physics papers and decided to have a quick early afternoon surf. There was no one else in the water. Most of the locals paddle out at dawn when the surf is at its best, but a gentle off-shore had been blowing all morning, and the two seventeen-year-old twins were hopeful.
    If you could send out a drone to take footage of the two teenagers, it would be an impressive sight. The coastline at Queensberry Bay on the East Coast of South Africa is particularly exotic. The bay is cupped by a point, with huge unspoilt dunes covered in sub-tropical coastal bush. The perfect backdrop for our extraordinary heroes.
    It was their contrasting skin colour that was so striking.
    Mila's was dark, close to black; her head was shaven and shiny, and she had striking large green eyes. Bonnie, on the other hand, was pearl white. Her long thick silver-blonde hair was tied in a plait down her back,

and she had the same green eyes as her twin. They were both in wetsuits, sitting on their surfboards, looking out over the Indian Ocean.

"I am so over matric," Mila said, "I can't decide if I am mostly bored or mostly terrified."

Bonnie smiled in agreement. She was more diligent than her sister and had set some ambitious academic goals. Still, the pressure was mounting and studying during their holidays was simply not fun.

Mila looked at her sister and was about to comment on the surf when Bonnie slowly slumped forward onto her board. It wasn't a collapse, just a slow-motion rolling forward - as if she was very tired or very sad all of a sudden. Mila paddled over to her in alarm.

"Bonnie! Bonnie! Are you ok?"

Bonnie looked up, but her eyes were glazed over.

"You are tuning into something, Bonnie. Let it go. Remember, you can't figure out what it is unless you can tune out first."

Bonnie's power and control as a telepath had strengthened over the past couple of years, but she was still caught off guard every now and then. Since age 14 she her ability to pick up people's emotions and bodily sensations had greatly increased in strength, but if she wasn't careful, she could get sucked right in.

Mila swam close enough to put her hand on Bonnie's shoulder. Gently, she helped her sister to sit up straight.

"Take a deep breath, sis. Balcony view, remember. Imagine you are looking down on yourself from a distance. Like we practised."

Bonnie looked into Mila's eyes and did as she was told, breathing slowly and deeply.

"I'm picking something up," Bonnie said, "but it is far away. Which is odd."

Usually, Bonnie's telepathy worked best in close proximity.

"Someone we know?" Mila asked, "Your connection is always stronger over a long distance if it is someone you are close to. Maybe it's Tess?" As Mila thought of her younger sister, her own heart skipped a beat.

Bonnie shook her head, "I don't think so?"

"Shall I clear a field?" Mila asked.

Madeleine Muller

Bonnie frowned at her sister. Mila's extraordinary ability to stop time was remarkable, but Bonnie also found it disconcerting. But they had noticed that Bonnie's ability to tune in over far distances was much greater when the whole world was quiet and suspended in a split second.

"It's like Professor Xavier's *Cerebro*," Mila said with a laugh, trying to keep it light. These days she moved comfortably between 'real time' and 'fake time' and more often than her sister suspected.

"I don't know," Bonnie started to protest, but before she could raise any further objections, Mila grabbed her twin's wrist with one hand and slowly brought the other one into a fist.

"STOP."

She said - and the world stopped.

The waves became still, and flecks of water and foam remained suspended in the air. Seagulls flying overhead looked like frozen statues; the wispy clouds across the blue sky stood motionless. Bonnie sat on the motionless board and experienced the strange feeling as if stepping on land after being on a boat. Mila smiled with satisfaction as she looked at her handiwork.

"There we go, sis. Time to figure out what was going on."

Ordinarily, Bonnie would argue with Mila about the willy-nilly use of her powers, but she was nervous. She had picked up something, just for a moment, but it was gone now. Bonnie pulled her legs out of the semi-solid water, which now felt like some strange rubber jelly, and folded her legs onto her surfboard. Mila gave her a reassuring smile and then lay back on her own board, enjoying the quiet and giving her sister a bit of space.

Bonnie took a deep breath and closed her eyes, sending her awareness over the waves towards the shore. She was searching for that same feeling of heaviness and weight that had engulfed her a moment ago.

"Got it," she whispered.

Mila watched her sister carefully out of the corner of her eye, but this time Bonnie seemed to be in control, a small frown of concentration furrowing her brow.

Superheroes in Sterkstroom

"It's Nina," she said with surprise.

"Nina?" Mila asked and sat up. "Little Nina in Keiskammahoek?"

Bonnie opened her eyes, "Yes. Except they aren't at Hog's Hollow. It's much further."

Mila nodded, "Yeah, that's right. Tess called this morning. The kids were all going to some nature reserve near Sterkstroom, not far from the Free State border."

"Really. Why? I didn't know...." Bonnie replied, sounding alarmed and confused.

Mila shrugged, "No big deal. Alex was taking them. I think they were asked to go see a sick animal. You know how Nina always helps out. But we didn't really talk about that. Tess was all excited about some new teenager on the farm called Indigo."

"And the new kid is with them? Who is it?" Bonnie's voice had raised a notch or two.

"Hey, chill out, sis. Just some volunteer on the farm. They are non-binary, so Tess was all 'enamoured'. She was hinting about some 'super-exciting' news to tell us, but you know Tess. It's probably something inane. This Indigo person is still at Hog's Hollow, looking after the horses. Let's get back to Nina, ok. What's happening?"

Bonnie tried to slow down her heart and make sense of what she had picked up. She had a soft spot for the quiet blonde thirteen year-old-girl.

"I don't know, Mila. It is as if Nina suddenly got very ill. Perhaps she had just tuned into a sick animal, but it was as if she were trapped in that space and didn't even know it. It was very off, though, like something was definitely not right. I'm worried."

Mila nodded, "Ok. Well, let's get the hell out of here and give Tess a call. Perhaps it was just a sick animal, and she is fine now. And if not, then we will go and see. Right?" Mila never hesitated when help was needed, no matter what it was.

Bonnie smiled at her sister, and a bit of colour returned to her cheeks. "Sure, good idea. Although if we need to go, I don't know how the hell we will get there. Sterkstroom, was it? And I would rather surf these waves to the shore than walk back on top of them, so can we please return to real time?"

Madeleine Muller

Mila gave her sister a wink, and the next moment Bonnie was knocked off her board as the swell suddenly surged back into motion.

"Hey," Bonnie shouted, but Mila was already coasting the white water back to shore. Bonnie shook her head in annoyance as she caught the next one in. By now, she would usually be laughing, but she couldn't shake the horror of that moment when she had tuned into Nina. Something was very wrong. She had felt so far away, so completely hopeless.

Please let Nina be ok.

Superheroes in Sterkstroom

Indigo

Chapter 12: *Indigo*

Indigo sat on the stoep of Hog's Hollow, nir hands cupped around a hot cup of chai tea.

This was definitely the life.

Ne had worked all afternoon with the horses and had that satisfying feeling of exhaustion after a productive day. Ne had forgotten how lovely it was to just spend quiet time with animals. At first, ne had been disappointed that nir new friends were heading off on their mission to Sterkstroom, but actually a proper holiday had been long overdue.

When Indigo's phone started buzzing on the small coffee table next to nir, ne felt tempted not to answer. Ne leaned forward to see the screen better, some number ne didn't know. But then curiosity overcame nem. Almost nobody had nir number.

"Hey, Indigo here."

"Hi. Indigo? Sorry to call out of the blue like this. My name is Bonnie. I am Tess' sister."

Indigo sat bolt upright, nir heart beating drums in nir chest.

What the hell?

The evening after their impressive rescue of Frau Kohler, Indigo had been thoroughly interrogated by Tess and had gladly admitted that the reason ne had come all the way to Hog's Hollow was because of nir search for other people like nem. Indigo confessed about the article and the twins, and although Tess did not say as much, she did not deny that her sisters had some sort of skill set. Beyond that, Tess had been all mysterious but had assured Indigo that she would put nir in touch with her sisters when they got back from Mpangwa.

Indigo wondered why Tess had given Bonnie nir number - and what exactly she had told her sisters.

"Ok?" was all Indigo could manage to answer.

"I'm afraid we need your help, or I wouldn't be calling like this. We have a little, well, situation on our hands. It has to do with Nina, Tess' friend…." Bonnie paused on the other end of the line.

"Is she ok?" Indigo asked, now thoroughly alarmed.

"Ja, sure," Bonnie said, but she didn't sound sure. Not sure at all. "Well, she is a little bit unwell. It's probably nothing."

Now Indigo was confused. Where on earth was this conversation going? Ne had a million questions but didn't even know where to start.

"I know you must have a million questions," Bonnie said, and Indigo felt a faint suspicion arise.

"Do you, now…." Indigo said, nir voice flat and on guard. Ne could hear Bonnie taking a deep breath on the other side.

"Ok. Let me stop beating around the bush. Tess told me about your skills and why you came to Hog's Hollow. And that you were hoping to meet up with Mila and me. Is that right?"

"Ja, that's right," Indigo said, trying to keep nir thoughts quiet and uninterested.

"Well, due to some new… developments, it looks like we might meet sooner rather than later. Or at least, I hope so."

"New developments?" Indigo prompted.

"Nina is sick," and with that, Indigo could hear the emotion in Bonnie's voice. "I don't know what it is, or if it is serious, or what is going on, but it is odd. Mila and I need to get to her, but we are only turning eighteen in October, so we have no driver's licence. I'm afraid this is a rather radical request, but we were hoping you could come and fetch us in East London and take us to Mpangwa. Just to be clear, it is going to involve a fair pack of lies to our parents and Aunt Jenni at Hog's Hollow, but there is no way that I can explain to anyone why Mila and I have to go."

Bonnie stopped, sounding out of breath. Indigo realised that the girl was close to tears. She must be in a real state to call up a complete stranger to come and help.

Bonnie continued, "We called Tess this afternoon to find out what was going on, and she suggested that we call you to help. I know you will be letting Aunt Jenni down…."

"No worries, I'm in," Indigo interrupted her. Ne had no doubts. Ne had always followed nir instincts, and those instincts had brought nem to this place and to this particular conversation. "I am embarrassed to say that lying is one of my special skill sets, Bonnie. When and where do I pick you up?"

Ne didn't ask for any more details. They would have more than enough time to talk in the car. Wasn't this exactly what ne was looking for? Even if all the twins wanted nem for was nir driving licence.

"Oh, thank you!" The relief in Bonnie's voice was palpable. "We will pay for the petrol and everything. We had hoped that you could come through early tomorrow morning. If you leave Hog's Hollow by 4.00 a.m., you can pick us up by six. We will tell my parents that Tess had invited us to come and stay at the nature reserve for a couple of days and that you are a good friend we met at camp or something that is visiting in town."

"Your parents going to let you guys get in the car with someone they have never met?" Indigo asked, bemused.

"Well, luckily, my dad's out of town," Bonnie laughed. "He is a real stickler. But my mom is lank cool. And she had wanted us to take a couple of days break during this holiday. Will Aunt Jenni be ok with you coming?"

"Well, to be honest, they don't actually need me. The old groom, Mr Sibeko, is more than capable. I stayed more for my own sake. I will just tell them I have to go earlier. No sweat."

"I don't know how we could ever thank you," Bonnie said, emotion again close to the surface. "It is probably nothing, but I just have to be sure. I will send you a location on WhatsApp, and then we will see you first thing tomorrow morning?"

"Sure," Indigo said, and then as an afterthought. "You have no idea how much I look forward to meeting you guys."

"Hundreds…." Bonnie replied. "Until tomorrow…."

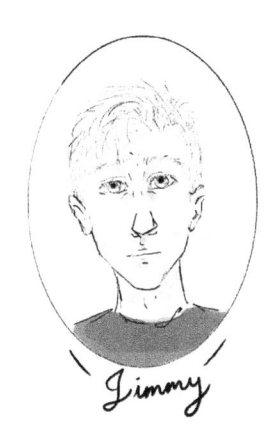

Chapter 13: *Jimmy*

Jimmy walked into the dining room at five minutes to seven. If it wasn't for Arno, he would have been late. When he was anxious, he tended to get distracted and always ran out of time. But Arno had pressed his suit, pushed him into the bathroom to shower well before time, and had plied him with Coca-Cola out of the mini-bar.

"The caffeine will do you good, honey," Arno had said whilst tying Jimmy's tie into what was apparently a full Windsor knot. But Jimmy was not so sure extra caffeine had been such a good idea. His heart was beating full gallop, and his palms were already sweaty.

As they walked towards the table, Jimmy gave Arno a quick look. He hadn't even noticed his friend getting ready but had to admit that Arno was a show-stopper tonight. He was wearing skinny black jeans ending in black Doc Martin boots with a descent-size chunky heel. With that, he sported a bright, voluminous, rainbow-blended coloured silk shirt in a French tuck that would have had Tan from Queer Eye smiling. Arno didn't walk, he glided, and Jimmy was sure that Arno was one hundred per cent more sophisticated in that silk shirt than Jimmy in his fancy-pantsy suit.

Madeleine Muller

It was midwinter and already dark outside. The thatch roof, red-brown tiles, face-brick walls and maroon table cloths made the room dark and intimate. Each table was crowned by a beaded lamp hanging from the beams in the roof, giving a semblance of privacy in the various circles of light. Outside it was chilly, but huge fires burned in several fireplaces along the walls, making it actually quite cosy.

Marthinus Brandt was already waiting, seated at a long table on the other side of the room. Next to him sat Dr Kuzmich, and Jimmy shivered involuntarily. The small, thin man was a head shorter than Jimmy and looked like a weasel. A hungry weasel. He must have just showered, his thinning hair plastered down, but small wet patches were already forming under the armpits of his khaki shirt.

As the boys arrived, the two men stood up. Old fashioned politeness, but Jimmy noticed the sneer with which Dr Kuzmich looked Arno up and down and felt his blood boil.

But at least his father was smiling.

"Good job, Arno," Mr Brandt said, nodding his head at Jimmy's smart suit whilst pointing to where they had to sit, "and nicely on time, too. You see, Igor, this is why I asked Arno to come. He understands appearances," and then addressing Jimmy and Arno again, "Kids, this is Dr Igor Kuzmich from the National Parks Board."

Jimmy nodded, wondering if his dad had forgotten they had met at the Shoal meeting, but Arno didn't miss a beat. He reached over the table with an outstretched hand, "Very nice to meet you, Sir. I have heard great things about you. Is it ok if I shake your hand?"

Jimmy looked at his friend in shock. An Oscar performance, if ever there was one. And with Arno so paranoid about COVID and all. For a moment, Dr Kuzmich looked as surprised as Jimmy, but then his face broke into a smile, showing off his nicotine-stained teeth, as he clasped Arno's hand in his.

"Well, I am not frightened of a little virus, young man. You say great things, eh? Yes, I can tell you I am turning things around at this pathetic little government department."

Superheroes in Sterkstroom

They sat down, and Arno nonchalantly splattered some of the hand sanitiser that was already on the table on his hands and offered it to Dr Kuzmich, who happily followed suit with a vigorous hand rubbing.

Jimmy felt himself calm a little. Arno was clearly running the show here.

"Well then," Marthinus said, his voice dropping to a conspiratorial whisper. "I'm glad you got here early. Mrs Braithwaite has confirmed that she is coming and is bringing Mr Dyani with her as well. She wanted to bring that blerrie Abongile, but I managed to deflect that little disaster. The plan is not to talk business tonight but to get the old lady on our side. Build a bit of trust. She is a nervous old biddy, so Jimmy, I want you to take care of her."

Jimmy felt Arno stifle a giggle next to him and knew exactly what his friend was thinking. Surely even his dad knows that in the business world, to 'take care of' someone can mean more than one thing. Mr Brandt must have noticed Arno's reaction,

"And that goes for you too, Arno. Be nice. It's the one damn thing you are good at."

"And picking out a good suit, Mr Brandt," Arno quipped with a bright smile, but Mr Brandt wasn't listening.

"Here she comes," he whispered almost in a panic, and the four men stood up in unison.

Jimmy turned round and watched with concern as the old lady carefully made her way among the tables, holding on to the arm of a short, stocky African man. She seemed small and ancient and withered. Jimmy guessed she weighed no more than forty kilograms, her clothes hanging loose on a spindly frame of bones. Her skin was wrinkled and dry, clearly from a lifetime of sun, and her long grey hair was plaited and rolled up in a bun at the nape of her neck. She didn't dress like an elderly woman and looked quite hip in khaki cargo pants and a khaki button-up shirt with a broach of a cheetah holding closed the top button. Jimmy wondered if she bought her clothes in the children's section, she was so small. The man, Mr Dyani Jimmy assumed, looked at her with concern. He was dressed in the same khaki outfit, and Jimmy realised that it must be some sort of uniform for staff at the reserve.

Madeleine Muller

"Mrs Braithwaite, how wonderful to see you," Marthinus boomed. "And my goodness, how sprightly you look. Not a day over fifty, I say." Jimmy felt uncomfortable with his dad's ridiculous flattery. She looked the very opposite of sprightly. Introductions were quickly made, and there was the usual confusion around whether to elbow bump, bow, or wave from a distance. No one shook hands. Mrs Braithwaite smiled politely, but Jimmy had the impression that this dinner was the last place she wanted to be.

Mr Brandt carefully manoeuvred the party to ensure that he, Dr Kuzmich and Mr Dyani were placed on one side of the table, with Mrs Braithwaite seated between Jimmy and Arno on the other side. He waved to the waiter to order drinks and spoke loudly and gregariously about the weather, about how lovely the reserve was and the style of the dining room.

Jimmy felt his heart sink. This was a disaster. Mrs Braithwaite was hardly replying, and Mr Dyani seemed distracted. The wine arrived, and for a moment, Mr Brandt drew breath as he poured them all a glass.

And then Arno spoke. He turned his body towards the old lady, looked her carefully in the eyes and said,

"*Hi, Tannie*[15], is something the matter? You look very sad." It was said with such sincerity and concern that the whole table literally froze. Old Mrs Braithwaite looked up from her plate for the first time, and to Jimmy's alarm, tears welled in her eyes.

"Ag, my boy. It's my pet, Nyama. He is very ill. I have been terribly worried about him, and I should really be looking after him tonight. Not attending this silly dinner."

"Shame, *Tannie*. No wonder you are so upset. Is it a little doggie? And what does the vet say?" Jimmy looked at his friend. This was not an act nor a nod to his father's instruction. This was just Arno being Arno. Mrs Braithwaite shook her head as she used the table napkin to dry her eyes.

"No, no. He is a cheetah. A beautiful creature. I have raised him since he was a cub. And the vet that usually helps us is in Queenstown and will

---

[15] Hey, Aunty

only be able to come next week. And I am sure by then it will be too late."

"A cheetah?" Arno gasped. "How precious. Oh, there must be a way to get him to a vet sooner."

At this point, Mr Dyani interrupted, "Now, Abigail, remember what I told you earlier. A vet is staying at the camp. She arrived this afternoon and will have a look at Nyama first thing in the morning. And Nyama ate a good supper tonight and is fast asleep now. There is nothing more you can do. Everything will be ok."

It was clear to Jimmy that Mr Dyani cared deeply about the old lady and would do anything to keep her happy. Mrs Braithwaite grabbed Arno's hand and held onto it tightly.

"Mzi is right. I mustn't' be so morbid. Nyama has had worse. It has just been a tough week. I must say that the beautiful shirt you are wearing is already cheering me up. What did you say your name was again?"

As Arno and Mrs Braithwaite launched into an intimate conversation about their favourite pets and animals, Jimmy noticed a look pass between his father and Mr Brandt.

It was the look of two crooks whose evil plot was going beautifully.

Jimmy shivered in revulsion. How was he going to survive this dinner?

Chapter 14: *Nina*

Nina woke up from her afternoon nap feeling groggy and disorientated. Tess was there, ready with a cup of rooibos tea and looking terribly worried. The concern on her friend's face helped Nina pull herself together. She was definitely feeling better, although she did not feel completely like herself.

"Hey you," Tess said, trying to keep the worry out of her voice, "You did a record nap there, girl. How are you feeling?"

Nina rubbed her eyes and smiled, "I am much better. Thanks. I'm sure I was just car sick or something. You look nice."

Tess had showered and was dressed in a clean denim dungaree-style dress with a red t-shirt underneath. Her unruly curly brown hair had been plaited into two plaits, and she was wearing a string of beads around her neck.

"We are going to have dinner at the restaurant with Abongile tonight. Alex said we have to clean up or at least put on a set of clean clothes. Ryan has been complaining loudly but has literally spent forever in the bathroom."

Nina giggled. Her friends were the absolute best.

Superheroes in Sterkstroom

"But we better hurry, Nina. You've got twenty minutes, girl. Alex has already gone for a predinner drink. We are meeting her and Abongile in the dining room."

After a bit of a rush, Nina had put on a long, white and blue patterned skirt and a long-sleeved navy blue cotton shirt. When Ryan met them in the living room, he let out a long whistle, "Hiert, my babes. Look's like we have a theme colour for K.I.D."

He did a little twirl, showing off his blue jeans, blue t-shirt and blue denim jacket.

Tess replied with a deadpan look, "I think I'm going to change." Nina laughed out loud, "Aaw, you guys look so cute!"

She grabbed Tess and Ryan each by the arm, and the three of them walked cosily in sync down the dirt road to the restaurant. The sun had set, and the air was cool and crisp. It almost felt a pity to have to go and sit in a stuffy, semi-dark restaurant. It took them a few minutes to find Alex and Abongile, who were already deep in conversation. Abongile stood up with a huge smile when he saw them approach,

"My three favourite detectives," he boomed and happily elbow-bumped each of them. Nina wished they could get back to a time when a hug wasn't such a terrible thing. "And how are you, Nina? Alex said you've been unwell."

"I'm fine, thank you," Nina said. "Thank you for inviting us to this beautiful place. It is a real treat."

They all sat down, and Abongile sorted out their drinks order. They were just about to get up to go and help themselves at the buffet when Abongile's eyebrows shot up, and he whispered, "That is her."

As one, all three children looked round and saw an ancient old lady dressed in the Mpangwa Nature Reserve uniform making her way through the restaurant. She was holding on to the arm of a stocky African man.

"She looks upset," Tess said. "Who is she?"

"That is Mrs Braithwaite," Abongile said. "It is her cheetah that is so ill. She is the owner of this place, and that man, Mr Dyani, is the manager.

Madeleine Muller

"Looks like they are meeting with someone," Alex said, and Nina watched as the old lady and Mr Dyani met with four men at a table on the far side of the restaurant.

Abongile snorted, "That is Mr Marthinus Brandt and Dr Igor Kuzmich. Brandt is the CEO of some company in Cape Town, and Dr Kuzmich is the new head honcho at the local National Parks Board. I don't trust either of them, and I can't figure out what the hell they are doing down in this neck of the woods."

"Who are the young guys?" Ryan asked. "The shirt that dude is wearing is awesome."

Abongile scoffed, "Well, the kid in the smart suit is Mr Brandt's son. Ran into him this afternoon. Shame. He is officially part of the firm, but I don't think he is having much fun. But the other kid…."

"Maybe it's his boyfriend," Tess added, and Nina agreed. He didn't look like the corporate type. He was chatting intently with the old lady, holding her hand, and Nina liked him already.

"Well, I don't trust them. Any of them," Tess said. "Do you think they have anything to do with the sick animals, Abongile?"

Abongile shook his head, "No, they are just vultures circling the dying prey, looking for a way to profit from this disaster. The extent of the disease in this area is too widespread and too varied. I don't think it is just one thing. My theory is that it is some sort of ecological disturbance. Humans interfere in so many ways with these sensitive ecosystems, what with our pollution and wasting of water supplies and natural resources. Maybe the system just couldn't take it anymore." And then he sighed, "Although I have never seen anything like this."

Tess shook her head, "But how could a big company possibly profit from a nature reserve that is dying?"

Ryan shrugged, "Maybe they want to use the land for something else and just want to buy it up cheap. Anyways. I'm starving. Let's get some grub."

And with that, Ryan jumped up to join the food queue. As they all made their way to the central table where the food was laid out, Abongile looked deep in thought. Nina heard him whisper to Alex, "The boy may have a point about the land having other uses. Might be worthwhile looking into."

Nina smiled with pride. They were not called the K.I.D for nothing. She was feeling much better, just thirsty and absolutely starving. The food looked delicious, and the next day, she was going to meet an actual cheetah. Things were looking up.

Madeleine Muller

Chapter 15: *Arno*

Arno picked out a long black skirt with a streak of rainbow running vertically down the one seam, a purple cropped t-shirt and his favourite purple lace-up boots. He ran his hands through the hair for that tousled bed-hair look and popped in a clip-in nosering. There would be no make-up today. This look had no need for embellishments.

Jimmy was still fast asleep. They had both been quite sensible with the drinks last night, even though Mr Brandt had been more than happy to ply them with wine, but Arno suspected it was emotional exhaustion that had knocked Jimmy out.

The two young men were staying in a rondawel with two single beds, and Arno had tried to be as quiet as possible as he got ready. Just before he left, he went to check on Jimmy, but his friend was still out. Arno looked down on Jimmy as he slept, curled up like a small child, innocent and perhaps even happy. Arno shook his head in dismay. And to think that, in reality, this was the evil *mafia boss'* son. Well, Mr Marthinus Brandt was not going to get away with whatever stinking plot he was brewing, not if Arno had anything to do with it.

Arno left a note for Jimmy on WhatsApp for when he woke and softly closed the door behind him. Luckily breakfast was served until 10.00 a.m., so there was no rush. He had made sure to ask about Nyama when they had said goodnight after dinner, and Mrs Braithwaite had invited Arno to come and see her favourite pet when the vet came to visit. He headed for the reception area. Mrs Braithwaite had told him to meet Susan in the lobby, and she would take him to her house. Arno was a bit nervous about intruding when the poor animal was being poked and prodded, but it had been too good an opportunity to pass up.

Mr Brandt had given him a pat on the back as they had left the restaurant, "Well done, Arno. Stroke of genius, my lad. You keep us posted."

Yeah, right. Arno thought. But his befriending of that poor old lady had nothing to do with Mr Brandt's evil plan. She had seemed so frail and vulnerable. And he had always wanted to see a real cheetah, even if it was a sick one.

Mrs Braithwaite's house was an impressive, lumbering thatch-roof house with a variety of intersecting rondawels and passages. The floors were covered in white tiles, and the walls were shades of pastel, lifting the darkness of the thatch. Beautiful pieces of art hung everywhere; otherwise, the house was minimalistic, giving the experience of walking through a gallery.

Susan led Arno through the house to the back and pointed to a door.

"They will be in there," she said and turned around to head back to the reception. Before she left, she put her hand on Arno's shoulder and whispered with wide eyes, "You are the most interesting person that has come to stay here this whole year." And then she was gone. Arno felt both flattered and slightly sorry for the girl. What a godforsaken place.

He could hear voices behind the door, and for a moment, he wasn't sure what to do. Should he knock? Call out? Or was he expected to just walk in? He opened the door a notch and peeked through.

It was an averaged-size round room, devoid of any furniture except for a huge dog pillow at the far end. It was crowded with people, but at that moment, his view was blocked out by a large black man yanking open the door. Arno looked up in awe. He had seen the ranger at dinner the previous night and had been impressed, but being this close to Abongile was completely overwhelming.

Madeleine Muller

"*Molo, Tata,*" He stammered, embarrassed and suddenly on the back foot.

Abongile looked Arno in the eye, not moving. He was blocking the entrance and seemed protective over those inside. He looked Arno up and down, and a vague look of confusion passed over his face. Arno used the gap, "I am looking for Mrs Braithwaite, *Oom*[16]. She said I could come and meet Nyama." Arno whipped out his best smile.

"Oh, is it Arno?" Arno heard Mrs Braithwaite's voice float up out of the room, and the next moment Abongile was pushed aside as if he was a feather. "Where is that boy of mine? Oh, look at you. What a lovely skirt. Abongile, this is Arno. He is a new friend of mine. Come in, dear child."

This was not the same frail old lady Arno had met the previous night. She was dressed in the same Mpangwa nature reserve uniform and had the same plait rolled up in a bun on her neck, but she stood tall and upright, and her eyes were clear and strong. She grabbed Arno by the arm in a pincher grip and dragged him into the room, "This is Alex, the lovely vet who has come to help. And there is my poor dear Nyama."

Arno noticed two things at the same time. The first was the beautiful but clearly ill cheetah lying on the large dog bed, surrounded by blankets, pillows, and toys. The other was the look of the lady vet sitting next to the animal, her blonde hair in a single plait down her back. She was furious and stared at him with such disdain he almost winced. Mrs Braithwaite didn't seem to notice. "And these are her three companions. Oh, you will have to remind me of your names. I have already forgotten."

Arno knew that Abongile and Alex, this vet lady, had been at dinner with a bunch of kids the night before but had not paid them any attention.

What on earth were they doing here?

A light honey-brown girl with two plaits, wearing shorts and a t-shirt stepped towards him. He guessed she was about thirteen, maybe fourteen years old, but she walked straight up to him and put her hand out, a huge smile on her face. A faint feeling of disquiet filled Arno.

---

[16] Uncle

Superheroes in Sterkstroom

"Hi, Arno, is it? My name is Tess. We are doing an elective with Abongile and Alex. This is Nina, and that is Ryan."

Arno shook her hand in a daze and was suddenly aware of how closed-in the space was with so many people in it. A positive COVID hotspot if ever there was one.

Nina, a girl with curly blonde hair, was standing at the dog bed, looking down at the cheetah. She didn't even look at Arno as she was introduced but seemed mesmerised by the beautiful creature, which in turn, seemed oblivious to all the people in the room. The boy, Ryan, was the exact opposite, coming right up to Arno and inspecting him with great enthusiasm. He even slightly lifted the hem of Arno's skirt and gave a low whistle, "Now those boots are *airie*, my bra. Hey Tess, now those are what I want for Krismis."

Tess rolled her eyes and pulled Ryan away, "I apologise for my friend. He is a bit rural," she said matter-of-factly. Ryan didn't seem to mind. She continued giving orders. "Mrs Braithwaite, perhaps you and Arno can go and make us some tea whilst we have a quick look at Nyama?"

Arno frowned. She was trying to get rid of him, the little minx. Something was up, and they wanted him out of the room as well as Mrs Braithwaite. And why was some kid bossing everyone around?

"That sounds like a good idea," the vet said, sounding all friendly and helpful, but Arno had not forgotten the look in her eyes earlier. He looked around, trying to get a feel for the room.

Where was the power here?

But perhaps going with Mrs Braithwaite would be the best bet. Isn't that why he came? To support the old lady? Maybe there is nothing more going on than these people trying to protect her from the pain of watching her favourite pet being prodded.

And then he noticed the girl, Nina.

She was still standing next to Nyama, looking down at the cheetah. Except she didn't seem to be looking at the animal - her eyes were glazed, and she was swaying. Everyone else's attention was on Arno and Mrs Braithwaite, and Arno was vaguely aware that they were about to be ushered out of the room.

Madeleine Muller

Suddenly, Arno watched Nina's knees fold, and with two steps, he was next to her, catching her in his arms as she collapsed in on herself. She was surprisingly light, but for a moment, Arno was off-balance. Thank goodness he hadn't worn his high-heeled boots. He steadied himself and gently kneeled down with the girl clasped to his chest. Her eyes were closed, and her breathing seemed strange and erratic. As he caught her, he heard shouts of alarm.

Alex reached them first.

"Nina! Nina! Are you ok?"

Arno looked down at the girl's face. She was out cold.

"I think she fainted," he said, but something told him that this was much more than just a faint.

"Here, let me grab a blanket," Abongile said. "Let's lay her down on the floor here." But then Tess spoke. That same bossy voice, but Arno could hear the anxiety in it.

'No. We need to get her out of this room, away from Nyama."

Alex nodded in agreement. Arno looked at the crowd surrounding him. Something was going on, and everyone was in on it - except maybe Mrs Braithwaite.

"Away from Nyama? Oh, my Nyama is completely safe," the old lady said. She seemed as confused as Arno felt. Arno noticed Tess and Alex exchanging glances before Alex spoke.

"Tess meant, to get her away from the cold floor. Perhaps you have a room with a bed we can lay her down on? She was a bit unwell yesterday. Probably just a faint, like the boy said."

And then Arno knew he didn't imagine things. This wasn't a faint. This was something else and had something to do with that cheetah.

"Oh, dear. The poor little thing," Mrs Braithwaite said. "Yes. Bring her to my room, of course. Shall I call an ambulance?"

"Good idea," Abongile said and reached to take Nina from Arno.

"All good," Arno said. "I've got her. She is very light. Just show me where I can put her."

And it was indeed easy to carry the slight girl. Arno had been working out this summer, and his body felt fit and strong.

Superheroes in Sterkstroom

As he followed Mrs Braithwaite and Abongile out of the room, Arno heard Tess whisper loudly to Alex, "We can't let Mrs Braithwaite call the ambulance. Bonnie and Mila are already on the road. They will be here just now. I think we should wait."

"It's too late," Alex whispered, "We can't just leave her unconscious."

But then Arno was out of Nyama's room and heading down the passage to the large, sparsely furnished bedroom of Mrs Braithwaite.

Arno was intrigued. Something was up. He looked down at the unconscious girl in his arms and felt filled with wonder.

Who is this person? What happened? And who are these people they were waiting for'?

As Arno laid Nina down on the bed, he noticed Mrs Braithwaite take her phone out of her pocket. He was sure that the vet and these other children cared deeply about Nina, yet they didn't want an ambulance. Was that enough to go on? Does he trust these people's judgement?

But Arno already knew the answer to that question.

Sometimes life was all about the greys, and sometimes the answer was clear as day. Just like Mr Brandt and Dr Kuzmich were the bad guys, these were clearly the heroes. He took a deep breath and said,

"I don't think it will be necess'ry to get an ambulance, Mrs Braithwaite. Nina woke up whilst I was holdin' her, and now I think she is just sleepin'. And she is burnin' up like anythin'. Wouldn't want to bother an ambulance for flu, hey?"

"Really? Oh, that is good," Mrs Braithwaite said, "but maybe we should just have her checked out."

"Oh, we can take her to the doctor's this afternoon," Alex said quickly. "Let us leave her to rest, and let me come and finish up with Nyama."

Mrs Braithwaite seemed only too happy to return to her pet, and soon the ranger, Alex and the old lady had headed back to Nyama's room.

Arno was left with Tess and Ryan, who were both looking at him carefully.

"Did she?" Tess asked, "Wake up?"

Arno shook his head.

"Why did you lie?" her voice was laced with suspicion.

Arno kept his own voice light.

"I heard you tell Alex you didn't want an ambulance. I assumed you had a good reason. I can see you really care about her. Was that right?"

Tess nodded, but tears were now running down her cheeks. She pushed past Arno and stroked Nina's hair.

"Nina. Nina. Can you hear me? Come back to us, girl. Just follow my voice. You are in too deep, Nina."

Just then, Tess's phone rang. She took it out of her pocket and passed it to Ryan without even looking at it. "It's probably Bonnie. Answer it will you. Ask her when they will get here."

Ryan looked at the name on the screen, "Yip. It's Bonnie, alright."

"Who is Bonnie?" Arno asked as Ryan answered the call.

"It's Tess' sister," Ryan said and then into the phone, "Howzit girl. How far are you guys?"

Although Arno couldn't hear exactly what Bonnie was saying, she was clearly upset and talking loudly. Ryan looked a bit wide-eyed, "Ja, but she was fine this morning, Bonnie. We just came and helped Alex with a sick cheetah, and then Nina just fainted."

Arno wondered if Tess had sent a message to her sister whilst he had been carrying Nina, although it didn't seem like there had been enough time. But it was clear that this *Bonnie* already knew that Nina was ill. Ryan looked towards the bed, "She's still out, hey. Tess is just having a look at her." And then a moment later, "Well, we didn't know, did we. She's usually A-ok with this kinda thing." After another minute of listening to Bonnie rant, Ryan finally rang off and sighed.

"They will be here in an hour. She said we should have waited. She's really pissed."

But Tess wasn't listening. She was sitting on the bed, holding Nina's hand, begging her to come back. Arno wondered from where.

Ryan, who had seemed like a complete goofball when they had first met, now took charge.

"Hey, Arno, my bra. You mind carrying Nina to our rondawel? Better that we meet the twins there. Tess will show you. I will go and tell Alex and Abongile and see what's happening with Nyama."

"No problem," Arno said. "Anything to help."

Superheroes in Sterkstroom

Arno was thoroughly intrigued. What was going on with Nina? And who were these twins?

Madeleine Muller

Chapter 16: *Nina*

Nina was lost. None of the landmarks seemed familiar. She was somewhere in the bush, with veldt stretching as far as the eye could see, dotted with acacia trees, aloes and wilde dagga. The sky was a pale blue, as if early in the morning, but there was no sun.

It was cold, terribly cold, and she was incredibly thirsty.

She couldn't remember how she got there or why she was there. She was disorientated and couldn't find her way. *And that noise.*

At first, Nina had been unaware of it, but now it seemed deafening. A high-pitched, scratchy uneven sound that came and went at irregular intervals. It had no rhythm or sequence, no specific melody - just noise.

A man-made sound, Nina thought and then she wondered why she thought that. The sound was making it hard to think, to figure out what was going on. She was supposed to be doing something… something important. Trying to remember anything was like having a word on the tip of your tongue, but each time she thought she knew what it was, that sound would singe through her brain.

She couldn't think.

Nina was lost. None of the landmarks seemed familiar….

Superheroes in Sterkstroom

Chapter 17: *Indigo*

At 10.00 a.m., Indigo, Mila and Bonnie arrived at the Mpangwa Nature Reserve gate. Indigo was out of breath with anxiety. The last three hours had been the most exhilarating of nir life.

*

Ne had picked up Mila and Bonnie at 6.00 a.m. sharp that morning, knocking on the door with nir heart beating in nir chest. The twins lived in a rather exotic setting in a small village right on the coast, the house hidden among the thick subtropical foliage.

Francesca Mgidi, the twins' Afrikaans mother, had opened the door, still wearing a thick cotton bathrobe.

"Good morning. You must be Indigo."

Francesca was smiling, but Indigo could feel the concerned mother inspecting nem carefully.

"*More Tannie*[47]," ne said in nir best Afrikaans. Languages had never been a problem for Indigo, even when nem wasn't shifting.

And just then, Bonnie pushed past her mom, Mila following close after. Indigo must have studied the photograph in the newspaper a hundred times and knew what to expect, but the two girls still took nir breath away.

---

[47] Good morning, Aunty

Madeleine Muller

Bonnie's gold-silver hair was plaited in a single plait down her back, her green eyes distracted and nervous, her pale skin soft and shimmering like moonlight. She slung her backpack over one shoulder and smiled briefly at Indigo as she headed past them towards the rental car. It was almost rude, but Indigo didn't mind. Ne had heard the sheer panic in Bonnie's voice the previous day.

Mila seemed much more relaxed and even this early in the morning had popped in a pair of large gold earrings and touched up her luscious lips with a spot of red lipstick, bright against her dark skin. Indigo wondered if her eyelashes were naturally that long or if she used extensions. Both the girls were wearing shorts and t-shirts, but where Bonnie's clothes were baggy and loose, Mila's shorts hugged her curves, and her skin-tight shirt left nothing to the imagination. Mila stopped in front of Indigo, dropped her bag and grabbed Indigo by the hand.

"Hey, bro. Long time no see, hey," and then Mila leaned forward and kissed Indigo loudly on the cheek. Indigo was suddenly aware of Francesca's scrutiny. They were all supposed to be old friends. Indigo didn't miss a beat.

"Gosh, Mila, Looking good, girl. And all dressed up this early in the morning. I'm impressed."

Mila rolled her eyes, "Tell me about it. But no matter the ungodly hour, one must always look one's best, hey. What can a girl do?"

Bonnie was loading her backpack into the boot of Indigo's rental car and looked up angrily.

"Come on, guys, let's get going. I want to get there before breakfast is finished."

Mila picked up her bag and headed for the car, and Indigo turned to Mrs Mgidi apologetically.

"*Jammer Tannie*[48]. Gotta go."

Ne worried briefly that the twins' mom would throw a last spanner in the works, but Francesca took a step back into the house and just waved goodbye.

---

[48] Sorry, Aunty

Superheroes in Sterkstroom

"Bye, girls. Have fun. Don't even think about your exams," and then to Indigo, "Drive carefully, please, and take it slowly on the N6. That road is full of potholes."

Indigo nodded and stood a little straighter, trying to look nir full eighteen years.

As Indigo had slid behind the wheel, ne had wondered what to say, but ne needn't have worried. Both Mila and Bonnie were full of questions, and soon they were all sharing their stories.

They had already left Cathcart far behind when Bonnie had her 'turn'. Mila was sitting in the front seat, with Bonnie in the middle backseat so she could share in the conversation. Indigo had just told them the whole story with Frau Kuhler when Bonnie's eyes suddenly glazed over. Indigo hadn't noticed until Mila put her hand on nir shoulder.

"Something's up with Bonnie. Pull over," was all she said. A long empty road stretched ahead, and Indigo swerved off the road and switched off the motor.

Bonnie spoke, her voice tinny and far away, "It's Nina. Something has happened."

"What?" Mila asked gently.

Bonnie shook her head, "I don't know. She is lost in the bush somewhere. I don't know."

Mila nodded and whipped out her phone, "You better call Tess, Bonnie. And Indigo, you better put foot, my friend."

*

The Mpangwa gate slid open, and Indigo drove into the nature reserve. It was a beautiful place, and there must have been good rain that summer, for the veldt was quite green for mid-winter. It looked different than the veldt Bonnie had described in her vision, but if Indigo understood it correctly, Nina wasn't actually in the bush but stuck in some dream.

Mila checked her phone, "Tess and Ryan have taken Nina to the rondawel they are staying in. It's called *Warthog*."

Although neglected, the place was well-signposted. They easily followed the little painted wooden signs, taking them straight there. They had not even gotten out of the car when Tess ran out through the front door. At the sight of her sisters, she burst out in tears and flung herself in Bonnie's arms.

"She is no better," Tess sobbed, "She just lies there."

Bonnie nodded grimly, gave her sister a quick hug and then headed inside. For a moment, Indigo was unsure if ne should join, but nir worry for Nina overcame nir fear. No way could ne wait outside.

Nina lay under the covers on the large double bed in the middle of the room. The curtains were drawn, and it was dark and cold inside, but even in the poor light, Indigo could see that Nina was way too pale. Ryan and Alex sat on the bed next to Nina, and in the corner of the room was some gorgeous young person in a skirt with a pride flag running down the seam.

Indigo was surprised at all the people there. Ne thought all this superhero stuff was supposed to be super secret. And although the vet knew about Nina, Indigo had been told that she had no idea of the twins' power.

As Bonnie sat down next to Nina, Alex got up and spoke,

"I am not sure about this. I mean, not calling the ambulance. Are you sure you know what the hell you are doing?"

Indigo realised that the poor woman was completely freaked out. But no wonder. She had brought Nina to Mpangwa to help, and something had gone dreadfully wrong.

"Keep cool, Alex. We've got this," Mila semi-commanded from the back of the room. "Let Bonnie do her thing." And then she spoke to Tess, looking pointedly at the guy in the corner, "Is he cool?"

Tess nodded, "I think so. He helped us get Nina here. Arno, are you cool?"

"Hundreds, sweetheart," was all he said, and Indigo recognised that tone of voice. He would do anything to not be excluded. Ne had been there before. Every queer's worst nightmare.

The room went quiet. Like the sound had been sucked out of it. Indigo found a chair in the back of the room next to the guy, apparently called Arno, and gave him a quick nod in greeting. Mila sat down on the bottom of the bed, and Tess climbed onto her lap, her long legs hanging down to the ground.

Bonnie closed her eyes.

Chapter 18: *Bonnie*

The first thing Bonnie noticed was the cold.

And the next thing was the noise. A scratchy, high-pitched noise that came and went at bizarre intervals.

She was standing in what looked like the surrounding veldt, but it was clearly a surreal landscape. A pale blue sky and no living thing in sight. Apart from that incessant noise, it was strangely devoid of any creatures. No birds. No insects.

A timeless dead place.

Nina, where was Nina?

Bonnie had helped Nina in the past when the little girl had been out of her depth whilst helping an animal. Last time the little girl had been sucked into the distress and pain of her beautiful horse, who had been ill with African Horse Sickness at the time[49]. But this felt different.

Bonnie turned to look in every direction, but the landscape was empty.

Best to start walking, she thought and shuddered. That noise was enough to drive one nuts.

She picked a direction and set off. It didn't matter which way she chose. In this place, there was no space and no time. It was somewhere in

---

[49] See *'Dimbaza Divine'*

someone's, or maybe something's, unconscious. It made no difference which way she went.

As she walked, the noise seemed to get louder, or was she just becoming more aware of it? She gritted her teeth.

Nina, where are you?

And then she saw something in the distance. A small, mustard-coloured bundle lying on the ground. She walked faster, and at first, it seemed like she couldn't gain on it at all, and then suddenly, she was next to it. It was the cheetah, Nyama. The old lady's pet cat.

The animal was lying down, panting, its eyes open but glazed over. Bonnie looked around, but she couldn't see Nina.

Think, Bonnie. This is not a place.

Bonnie knelt next to the cheetah and started stroking it. Its pelt was impossibly soft. It was looking at her now, its eyes pleading. Bonnie took a deep breath and closed her eyes.

When she opened them, the world had changed. It was dark, and although it was the same veldt, it was filled with mist, the air thick with humidity. The sound was still here, but much softer... muted. Nina was next to her, in exactly the same spot the cheetah had been lying. She was curled up in a foetal position, her eyes tightly closed.

"Nina," Bonnie said softly. "Nina, sweetheart. I am here. I've come to fetch you."

Nina's eyes opened and looked at her searchingly.

"Are you really here?"

Bonnie smiled, "Well, that is a tricky question. Are either of us really here? But yeah. I am in your room. Here at the Mpangwa Nature Reserve."

"Nyama?" Nina asked.

"Don't worry about Nyama now," Bonnie said. "Time to wake up. Tess is in a complete state."

"There is that terrible noise," Nina said. "I can't think in that noise."

Bonnie nodded. She had only been experiencing this world second-hand. It must be ten times worse for Nina.

"So let's get out of here. What do you say?"

Nina nodded, "But how?"

Madeleine Muller

"Come," Bonnie said and stood up, holding out her hand. Nina took it and allowed herself to be pulled upright. Bonnie gave her a quick hug. Nina's skin was freezing cold; she needed to move.

Still holding Nina by the hand, Bonnie started walking, then broke into a gentle run..

"But we can hardly see anything," Nina protested in alarm. Bonnie laughed.

"What's the worst that can happen, Nina, a scraped knee?" With relief, Bonnie saw Nina give her a smile in return, now easily jogging next to her.

"Always better to be doing something," Bonnie said, picking up the speed, "even when you are not going anywhere. Even when it makes no sense."

Nina nodded, and Bonnie's heart contracted. She was giving superpower lessons, but Nina seemed too young to be having to face stuff like this.

It felt like they had been running for only a second.
It felt like they had been running forever.
The sound was everywhere, yet there was no sound.

And then they were falling as if the ground had simply given way.

"What's happening," Nina screamed.

But Bonnie was laughing, "We are waking up, Nina-pie. Hold on."

Chapter 19: *Jimmy*

Jimmy looked at his phone in annoyance, but still no message from Arno.

The last message displayed on his phone was the one Arno had sent early that morning when he had slipped out on his little mission to Mrs Braithwaite. Jimmy vaguely wondered whether he should be worried, but he didn't think either Mrs Braithwaite or her dear cheetah were a threat of any kind. The most dangerous person on the bloody property was that horrible Dr Kuzmich. Or worse still - his dad. Jimmy sighed.

He ended up having breakfast alone, which was a bit of a worry, for Arno's favourite thing in the world was a full breakfast buffet. At least there had been no one else in the dining room - neither his dad nor that scary ranger had made an appearance.

Jimmy looked at his watch. They had a meeting scheduled with Mrs Braithwaite at 10.00 a.m., a mere ten minutes away. Although Arno was not part of this official meeting, he was supposed to help get Jimmy ready.

Jimmy sighed again. But that was not really true - for Arno had already prepared everything. Jimmy's suit had been pressed and neatly hung up before Arno had left. He had placed a new clean shirt and tie on the bed, specially handpicked. Jimmy imagined Arno tip-toeing around the room that morning whilst he was sleeping, polishing his shoes and ironing the shirt. He wished Arno had woken him up. He felt like he had gotten out of the wrong side of the bed that morning. Arno was his pick-me-up, his cheerleading team, his BFF... He couldn't start his day without Arno.

Jimmy managed to get to the Mpangwa Nature Reserve boardroom by 10.05 a.m. Arno would have been impressed, but his dad still gave him the beady eye. Mr Brandt and Dr Kuzmich were already seated at the large wooden boardroom table, laptops open and plugged into the central console, their presentation loaded. Jimmy smiled nervously and sat down.

What was the big deal? Mrs Braithwaite wasn't even there yet.

She arrived a few minutes later with Mr Dyani in tow. This morning she did not seem as frail as the previous night but rather flustered and anxious.

"Good morning, gentlemen. I am so sorry to have kept you waiting. We have had a bit of a kerfuffle this morning."

Jimmy cleared his throat, "How is Nyama, Mrs Braithwaite. What did the vet say?" Although he was oddly more anxious about what happened to Arno. Jimmy noticed his dad giving him a look of approval. His old man had probably completely forgotten the reason for the old lady's distress.

"Oh, thank you for asking, my child," Mrs Braithwaite said as she sat down. "He is not much better, I'm afraid, although the vet took some bloods, and we will have to wait for the results. I am a bit more reassured now that a professional is looking after him. But unfortunately, her little assistant, Nina, took ill and fainted."

And then she turned to Jimmy, putting her hand on his shoulder. "Your friend caught her as she fell and carried her to my room. That Arno is such a dear boy."

Jimmy smiled and nodded. Arno was certainly a dear boy, and he guessed that is what caused the delay. It sounded like Arno had saved the day.

During the next hour, Jimmy struggled to look interested as his dad took Mrs Braithwaite and Mr Dyani through their presentation. Jimmy knew it by heart as he had helped with the slide design and the graphics. It was mostly a financial breakdown of the current challenges Mpangwa was facing and how Marthinus Brandt planned to save the day. Lots of fancy graphs and pie charts. Of course, there was no mention of fracking or oil exploration, and the 'vision" was all about nature preservation and revitalising the business. Arno would call it Class A *BS*, with sprinkles on top.

Mr Brandt finished his presentation, "As you can see, there is lots of potential, but it will need a large cash injection and, unfortunately, a small enterprise such as your own cannot possibly raise the necessary funds. At least the Brandt Corporation can ensure that your dream continues to live on."

Jimmy stifled a yawn and happily hid behind his mask.

There was a short but slightly uncomfortable silence as Marthinus finished. He had a stupid smile stuck on his face as if he had just delivered a rather large and overpriced gift.

Mr Dyani and Mrs Braithwaite gave each other a meaningful look, and then Mr Dyani asked, "Mr Brandt, this all sounds very smart, but what we don't understand is why you don't simply come in as a shareholder and invest in our business? We are happy to work with you and implement some of these strategies if you think it would help, but why is it necessary to buy us out completely?"

Mr Brandt nodded a couple of times as if seriously considering the question, but Jimmy knew his father was ready for this one.

"I did suggest this very idea to my company, Mr Dyani. But I am afraid that although I think this place has potential, not everyone agrees. What we are attempting to do, to return this place to profitability, is going to be very difficult. And I have to be honest, there is a risk of failure. And if we fail, then my funders want to have some sort of surety."

"Meaning the deed of this property," Mrs Braithwaite said. Mr Brandt shrugged,

"We are hoping it won't come to that. But just like any bank giving a loan, there needs to be some way of recouping our investment in case things don't work out. It is very unfortunate, I know."

"And what about the staff and the Cooperative?" Mr Dyani asked.

Madeleine Muller

Mr Brand rolled out his winning smile, "I am sure we can make a plan and come to some sort of agreement. As long as the reserve keeps going, we will need people to run it, will we not?"

Jimmy felt slightly nauseous. His dad was not planning to 'run' this reserve for maybe more than a few months. The sale to Shoal was already pretty much a done deal. He just needed Mrs Braithwaite to sign the deal and get the property in his company's name.

Mrs Braithwaite sighed and sat back, "I don't know, Mr Brandt. Financially it is a very attractive deal and will certainly ensure a better future for Mpangwa. But letting go of this place causes me much distress."

Mr Brandt nodded sympathetically, "Of course, I understand. And you can live here as long as the reserve is running. And by all means, discuss it with your staff and the Cooperative. We only need an answer by the time we leave here."

Jimmy knew they were leaving in a couple of days, an unreasonably short time to make such a huge financial decision. He vaguely hoped Mrs Braithwaite had a good lawyer or accountant or someone that would go through this deal with a fine tooth comb, but he doubted it.

They all stood up to leave.

"Let us know how Nyama is doing, Mrs Braithwaite," Jimmy said. "Once you have those results."

Mrs Braithwaite gave a wan smile, but Jimmy could see the weight of this decision was weighing her down. He suddenly had a vision of Mrs Braithwaite being forced to pack up her house and leave once his dad had sold the property.

Where would she even go?

Jimmy shuddered. *Arno was right. This should not be allowed to happen.*

Jimmy looked at his dad and Dr Kuzmich. They seemed full of confidence and were surely congratulating themselves on a successful meeting. A cold shiver ran down his back.

But what could he do? What would his dad do if he found out Jimmy had somehow sunk his deal? Jimmy felt a ball of anxiety clench his stomach, and powerlessness overcame him.

How could he fight his dad?

Chapter 20: *Arno*

Arno had never experienced a room full of people so quiet. It was as if they all held their breath, watching Bonnie and Nina. He struggled to keep from jiggling his legs, wracked with anxiety. Usually, he was the centre of the room, the most 'interesting' person there, as poor Susan attested.

But not today.

Today he had definitely been eclipsed. Not that he minded - this was the coolest thing that had happened to him all year - but he felt out of place and discomfited, like he was supposed to do something but didn't know what.

When he had heard about the the two sisters, the twins, he had assumed they would have the same brown skin as Tess, but instead, three people had arrived, and they were nothing like he expected. It had taken him a minute to figure out that the very light-skinned girl with the blonde hair was Bonnie, now sitting with her eyes closed next to Nina on the bed. Her sister Mila was the dark one, gorgeous and exotic as a cocktail, but with the same clear green eyes. The bond between the three sisters was clear, Mila like a protective bodyguard, sitting at the end of the bed with long-legged Tess on her lap.

But he hadn't expected a third person - no one had mentioned them. He didn't know their name, but they had a small trans flag on the pocket of their short denim jacket, and when they sat down, they gave him a quick nod of understanding.

One queer to another.

They were extraordinary. A good head taller than the twins but carrying their height proudly. Thin and strong, with a Mediterranean colouring – short pitch-black hair, olive-coloured skin, and eyes dark and piercing. They were dressed in stone-washed jeans, a black t-shirt and black Doc Martins. Arno was in complete awe. He had long forgotten about Mr Brandt's evil plots and investigative schemes. Like everyone else, he kept vigil over the small little girl in the bed and the pearl-white angel holding the child's hand, her eyes visibly moving behind her closed lids.

Arno had no idea how long they waited, maybe a few minutes - perhaps as long as half an hour.

And then, suddenly, Bonnie gasped and opened her eyes. She quickly scanned the room as if orienting herself to her surroundings and then looked down at the child.

"Nina," she whispered, and Nina's eyes flew open with the same startled gasp as Bonnie had given a second earlier. The room broke into a cacophony of relieved sighs and chatter. Tess got to Nina first, and everyone had to hug her and check on her and was laughing and crying and hugging each other. Even Arno's eyes welled up, and he had never even met the girl. He stood up and found Abongile towering next to him, one eyebrow slightly raised. Was Abongile going to ask him to leave? But Abongile simply asked,

"Do *you* have any idea what just happened?"

Arno shook his head. Abongile looked at his watch, "I need to go. Alex and I are supposed to be meeting up with Dr Kuzmich."

Arno tried to look as if he were part of the team, "Looks like these twins have got it under control…."

Abongile nodded, and Arno added as an afterthought, "Abongile, watch out for Dr Kuzmich."

Abongile turned his attention back to Arno, "And what exactly am I looking out for."

Superheroes in Sterkstroom

"Just don't believe a word that china says. Any claims he makes - get them double-checked like, ok?"

Abongile nodded, "Thanks, kiddo. Must say I have never liked the man. You know something?"

Arno swallowed. *Where exactly did his loyalty lie?*

"Jimmy is my best friend, and I have his back, my bra. So I am going to hold back for now if that is ok."

Abongile gave Arno a warm smile and put a large hand on his shoulder, "Sure. Loyalty is a good thing. You look after your friend, but let me know if I can help at any time. How does that sound?"

Arno smiled back and realised how unsettling it had been trying to figure out this scheme with Mr Brandt on his own. Having someone on their side suddenly made him feel just a little bit safer.

Alex gave Nina a last hug before she set off with Abongile, and Arno was left with six of the most interesting people he had ever met! And to think, they were all younger than him - although perhaps the three older kids not by that much.

And at that moment, all of their attention turned to him.

Ryan did the introductions, first running round the bed to take Arno by the arm, like a proud show and tell.

"Nina, this is Arno. He was your *ridder op a wit perd*[50], my girl. It was him that caught you when you fell down." And then a slight look of worry crossed his face, and he asked, "Or are you non-binocular like Indigo?"

Arno's mouth literally fell open, and the whole group burst out in laughter, Indigo the loudest.

Tess interjected, with both laughter and slight annoyance in her voice, "Good grief, Ryan. It is non-binary. I'm going to have to tattoo it on your bloody forehead."

"Now I won't be able to see it if you put it on my forehead, now would I, hey? Maybe we should rather tattoo it on yours.?" Ryan retorted sharply, and Arno thought it best to interject.

---

[50] knight in shining armour (lit knight on a white horse)

Madeleine Muller

"No, it's fine. He /him is cool. Although I don't really mind which pronouns you use, bra. A bit gender fluid, I guess, but even that is quite fluid. Happily queer, you know…." And suddenly, he blushed. Although he outed himself daily with how he dressed, he never talked about his identity. Certainly not in Hanover Park, not even to Jimmy. But he had never met a group of people so completely openly accepting of who he was and what he might represent. Arno swallowed, suddenly at a loss for words. Indigo put their hand on his shoulder.

"No worries, bro. With this lot, we are the average Joes for a change. I'm Indigo, by the way," and then turning to the group, "Now that introductions have been done, I would very much like to hear why I have just driven Bonnie and Mila a couple hundred kilometres to this godforsaken place."

Chapter 21: *Tess*

Tess flipped open her notebook and did a quick scribble in the corner to check that her pen was working. She was sitting on the front stoep of their rondawel at the head of a long cast iron table with cold, cast iron chairs. Tess had found some cushions stashed in an impressive large wooden chest, whilst Mila had sorted out Nina with food and water. She had returned from her sleep, or coma or whatever it was, desperately hungry and thirsty. Bonnie seemed ok, just slightly tired, and Tess was feeling nervous. It was time to start figuring out what was going on.

Bonnie had given them a quick description of the world she had found Nina in. As Tess understood it, Nina had been trapped in Nyama's unconscious.

But what was happening with Nyama? And was this the same thing that was happening to all the other animals?

Everyone found their seats, and Tess looked at her compatriots with a sense of satisfaction. There were seven of them, a perfect number for a team of superheroes, or at least superheroes and their sidekicks. She still had reservations about Arno, but somehow he seemed to be a good fit for the team.

And they did have Bonnie, who would sniff out spies or traitors at the drop of a hat.

Tess cleared her throat, "Great, everyone. I think we need to go through this morning's events step by step and see what we know...."

Ryan interrupted, "And why are you chairing the meeting, hey? I think Mila should be in charge."

Mila was lounging back in her chair as usual, but now she leaned over the table and roughed up Ryan's hair (if it were even possible to rough up his unruly curls any further), who was sitting opposite her.

"Chill, Ryan. I vote for Tess as chair. Look, she even has a notebook."

Ryan glared at Mila, but before he could reply, Nina, sitting next to him, put a hand on his shoulder.

"Let Tess do the organising, Ryan. That's her superpower."

Tess gave Ryan a small smile of victory and continued, "Nina, can you explain to us what this place was like? Any clues as to why Nyama is so ill?"

Tess looked at her friend and felt her heart beat faster. Nina looked small and frail, with dark shadows under her eyes. Her voice, when she spoke, was just above a whisper.

"It's hard to explain, Tess. Usually, when I tune in, I can feel what the animal feels and see what the animal sees. But this time, it was different. It was like Nyama was trapped somewhere else."

"You mean he tuned into somewhere?" Mila asked.

"No," Nina replied, "Like he had been caught by something. It has something to do with that noise. It was terrible."

"What noise?" Indigo asked,

Bonnie answered, "I hadn't mentioned it yet, but there was the most bizarre sound in that place. It was irregular and high. It was a horrible sound - really unsettling."

Nina continued, "It completely scrambled my thoughts. I couldn't think straight. It made me feel really unwell. That's why I couldn't get out. I can't imagine living with that sound all the time. Maybe that is why Nyama is so unwell."

Mila nodded slowly, "Alex mentioned that she couldn't figure out what was wrong with the cheetah. There was nothing she could put her finger on. The blood tests may give some answers."

Superheroes in Sterkstroom

Tess wrote all this down in her notebook, "Do you guys think that the sickness that Nyama has might be the same sickness that is affecting the other animals?"

"We need to go and find out," Nina said, suddenly looking alarmed and worried. "Abongile could take us out on a game drive…."

"Whoah," Bonnie said, "You are not tuning into another animal. Certainly not anytime soon. We are not doing that again."

Mila was nodding in agreement.

But Nina was shaking her head adamantly, "I know this is crazy, but this is exactly why I am here. We need to find out if the other animals are experiencing the same thing. I am the only one that can tell. And this time, I won't be caught off guard. And Bonnie is here."

Tess took a deep breath, "Nina is right. We don't even have to check a lot of animals. Even just one would confirm it. We can't fix this if we don't know what is going on."

Arno suddenly cleared his throat, "Sorry to interrupt. But I was wondering. This sound. Did it sound like a natural sound, even if distorted, or was it a man-made sound? Did a person or animal make it, or a machine?"

Tess looked at Arno with interest. She could see where he was going with this. That was a very good question.

Nina did not hesitate, "I did wonder, but I think it was definitely not a natural noise. It was like bad morse code with some static, maybe. But no, it was not a sound you hear in nature. Certainly not a sound made by an animal."

Bonnie nodded in agreement and confirmed what Tess was thinking, "Which means it might be an actual sound out there somewhere - a sound made by a machine."

Mila gave a low whistle, "And animals can pick up all kinds of sounds that humans can't hear. Imagine if that noise is actually out there all the time; surely that would explain a lot."

Tess tapped with her pen on her notebook, "Well, first we have to confirm that by finding some more of these ill animals. And then the next question is, what is causing such a sound? Is it part of some noise pollution, a broken or malfunctioning machine or…."

Madeleine Muller

Tess paused, and Arno finished her sentence, "… or is someone doing this intentionally?"

Chapter 22: *Nina*

The road was bumpy, and Nina was jiggling around like a sack of potatoes. She felt nauseous, even with all the fresh air in the twelve-seater open-sided four-by-four safari vehicle, which was carefully picking its way over the potholed dusty road. Abongile was driving, although it had taken a lot of explaining to convince him to take them out into the bush after Nina's turn that morning. They had decided to let him know about Nina's ability to tune into animals, although Nina was sure that he only believed them because Alex had confirmed their story. But both Abongile and Alex had been sceptical about the sound Nina described.

Abongile had shaken his head, "*Hayi bantwana*[51], you are telling me there is some ghost sound out there?"

Alex had also been puzzled, "I've never heard of illness being caused by sound…."

But still, here they were, driving out to the nearby dam on the reserve, a good place to find some wildlife.

The further they drove into the bush along the windy, grassy track, the worse Nina felt. Her limbs were heavy and achy, and she worried she might throw up. Tess kept giving her concerned looks, and Nina perked

---

[51] **No, children**

up and smiled - trying to not look as bad as she felt. She worried they would turn back if they knew how ill she felt - and she had to do this. She could still feel the horror of Nyama's distress.

Was the sound caused by Nyama's illness, or was it an actual sound out there that other animals were also being exposed to?

They had to figure out what was going on.

The Mpangwa Dam was set in a valley amongst a circle of hills, with thick bushes along its edges. Little animal footpaths snaked down to the edge of the water.

"Any crocodiles?" Ryan asked, sounding both excited and terrified.

Abongile laughed, "This isn't the jungle, Ryan."

"And you are not Indiana Jones," Tess added.

"Ag, come on now," Ryan replied with mock petulance. "Be nice."

Abongile turned to the group, "We made a lot of noise getting here, so most of the wild would have run off or will be in hiding. From now on, dead quiet, please. Let us start by scouting this side of the dam...."

Tess interrupted, "I think Nina should lead the expedition."

Nina blushed, embarrassed to contradict Abongile, but she knew Tess was right and added matter of factly, "I can find the animals that are hiding."

Abongile looked momentarily deflated but then stepped back.

"*Kulungile*[52]," he said, "lead the way."

It didn't take them long to find the shrub hare. Nina had only taken a few steps down the pathway when she felt its presence. And they did not have to worry about it running away - the shrub hare was lying next to a thick clump of grass, exposed and with eyes glazed. It was still alive, but barely.

Nina looked nervously at Abongile. She wasn't sure she could do this with all these adults watching. But Bonnie understood.

The pale girl turned to Alex and Abongile, "Nina is going to need some space to do this. And I can help her. I know how to get her back if she tunes in too deep. Perhaps you could see if there are any other sick animals around...?"

---

[52] OK.

Superheroes in Sterkstroom

"We'll come and help," Indigo said, including Arno in the offer, and Arno nodded.

Abongile looked uncertain, but Alex agreed, "They are right, Abongile. We can't help here. Why don't you and I go round the left of the dam, and Indigo and Arno can go round the right. I want to get an idea of the types of diseases in the reserve and the kinds of animals affected. A shrub hare is very different from a cheetah…."

Nina watched them go and felt a sense of relief. Not the kind of thing you want to do with an audience, but also not the kind of thing you want to do alone. Her four friends were looking at her attentively. Mila had stepped back, like she was standing guard. Ryan had sat down on his haunches, chewing on a long piece of grass and Bonnie and Tess was right next to her. Nina smiled, "It's going to be fine. I know what to expect now."

Bonnie stepped forward, "I will go in with you this time. And we stay as short a time as possible."

Nina nodded and kneeled down next to the hare. It was a young one, almost an adult. It was breathing very fast. Nina could tell that the hare was aware of them but was too unwell to react. Gently she stroked it, sending out messages of safety. She could feel it calm a bit.

Time to tune in.

Nina closed her eyes and felt Bonnie's hand on her shoulder. It was a strange feeling, stepping into the hare's experiences with a passenger.

The first thing Nina noticed was the sound. That same terrible sound, but much louder now. It was even more overwhelming than with Nyama. She shuddered and felt Bonnie's hand squeeze her shoulder. Was that squeeze out there in the veldt or in here in the nothingness?

The next thing she noticed was the landscape.

For a moment, it seemed strange and even more surreal than Nyama's dream. It was still veldt, but the proportions were all wrong. It took Nina a moment to remember that she was seeing it from a shrub hare's perspective. The grass was much higher, the trees huge overhead, and her awareness was more of the ground and its burrows than the vast skies above. The light was different but still had that same eerie, dead quality.

Madeleine Muller

But that sound felt like it was building and building, searing Nina's brain. Nina put her hand over her ears but couldn't block it out. Her nausea increased, and she felt her knees getting weak.

"Time to go," a voice whispered in her ear. It was almost impossible to hear it over that noise.

"Nina!" the voice said, much louder now, and Nina felt like pushing it away from her. She needed to find a way to block this noise.

"Open your eyes, Nina. Now!"

The voice was commanding, urgent. Nina felt confused. Her eyes weren't closed, were they? For a moment, she shut them, but this simply amplified the sound more than ever.

When she opened them again, she was still in the strange veldt, but a girl was in front of her, a pale girl with blonde hair - looking straight into her eyes.

"Time to go!" the girl commanded and slapped her.

The slap was not very hard, but Nina felt as if she had tripped and was falling backwards. Falling and falling.

And then she was lying on the grass, a clear African sky above her as well as four concerned faces. The noise was gone.

"You ok?" Tess asked, visibly spooked.

Nina wanted to reassure them, but she felt so close to vomiting that she couldn't risk speaking.

"Sit her up," Mila said, "She looks positively green."

Nina felt hands pick her up and prop her against a nearby *Knobkierie Tree*. Her eyes welled up with tears, and she grabbed Mila's arm.

"Mila. Please. The shrub hare. It's that noise - it's terrible, and the poor thing is suffering. Please can you help? Like you did with Toast when he was ill? Just until we figure this out? I can't make it go away. We can't leave the poor animal like this."

Bonnie looked at Mila, "That's actually a good idea. If you could freeze it in a time bubble, it should give it some relief from the noise for the time being. Just like that time you slowed down Toast's illness."

Superheroes in Sterkstroom

Nina had seen Mila in action before, and that was over a year ago.[53] It had always been easy for her to grasp Bonnie's powers - Bonnie could tune into people as Nina could tune into animals - but Mila's skill set was way more mysterious.

Mila could manipulate time, or as Tess described it, take things "out of time." When Nina's dear Palomino horse, Toast, had come down badly with African horse sickness, Mila had placed it in a time bubble, freezing it in a split second, giving time for the medicine to arrive before the animal was too sick to be helped.

"But we can't leave it here, like," Ryan added. "It will make a nice little *happie*[54] for a passing hyena. I'm surprised it's not been picked up already."

Mila stepped forward, "Let me wrap it up and get it some temporary relief, and then we are going to have to make a plan. Remember, this shrub hare might not be the only one."

Nina was starting to feel a bit better. Bonnie had placed the shrub hare on her lap, and she was gently stroking it, using the last bit of her energy to calm it. She watched in fascination as Mila bent over the little creature, holding the palm of her hand about ten centimetres above the hare. Her lips were moving, but Nina couldn't hear what she was saying. The creature went completely still, with no breath, no heartbeat, and no distress. Although Nina had not been tuning in, she could still feel its relief.

She smiled at Mila, and tears ran down her face, "Thank you, that is much better."

Bonnie asked, "Nina, does this mean you are being affected by what is happening to the hare, even when you are not tuning in?"

Nina frowned, "Perhaps. Although that's not usually a problem…."

"But we don't know what we are dealing with," Bonnie said, "Maybe we should get you home, Nina. Away from this reserve."

Nina shook her head vehemently. She was getting tired of being babied, "I'm fine, dammit. Please let me help. I need to solve this! I'll be fine."

---

[53] See 'Dimbaza Divine'
[54] morsel

Mila gave Bonnie a quick look and then sat down next to Nina and took her hand, "Don't worry, Nina. *We* will solve this. You have got a great team here, remember? And we always have time."

Jimmy

Chapter 23: *Jimmy*

Jimmy was sitting in the public lounge, drinking his second cup of coffee and re-reading the WhatsApp message. He was trying not to get irritated.

> Hey, bra. Going on a game drive with the ranger and the kids. Later.

Wasn't this what they agreed on? For Arno to find out more about what is going on? But Jimmy felt left out and jealous of all these new friends Arno had made. And anyway, a game drive sounded like super fun.

They were running out of time. Once Mrs Braithwaite signed that deal, that would be that. And how exactly was Arno's investigation into the ecological crisis with all those sick animals going to help?

Perhaps it was time to have a talk with his father. Jimmy shuddered at the thought. But that would be the grown-up thing to do. If he had concerns about this deal, he had to approach his dad man-to-man, not any of this skulduggery. But even just thinking about his father caused his heart to gallop in his chest. Jimmy took a few deep breaths and closed his eyes. He needed a plan.

Just then, Jimmy jumped as Marthinus Brandt's voice thundered across the room, "Ah, there you are, James! Been looking all over for you. Are you asleep?"

Jimmy sat bolt upright, stuttering in surprise as if being caught out for slacking on the job. "N…n…no, Dad. I'm just having some coffee."

"Good idea," Mr Brandt said and headed over to the coffee machine to pour himself a cup. Jimmy looked at his father nervously. He clearly had something on his mind. Mr Brandt sat down and gave Jimmy one of his winning smiles that he usually kept for sales meetings. Jimmy gave a half-smile back. Luckily, his dad could not read others; he was your typical male bull in a china shop.

"So what is Arno up to?" his father asked nonchalantly.

Jimmy took another sip of coffee to give himself a second to think. He had to be careful. His dad was happy with Arno hanging out with Mrs Braithwaite but might not be so happy about him being on a game drive with the Green Scorpions. Jimmy also knew that Susan had the afternoon off.

"I think he has gone off with Susan somewhere. You know how he likes to make friends."

Marthinus Brandt nodded slowly as he digested this, "Hmm. Didn't think she was his type."

Jimmy thought it best not to answer. Let his father lead the conversation on this one.

"You see, son," Mr Brandt said, "His help would be greatly appreciated. Mrs Braithwaite is so close to signing; she just needs the last bit of prompting from someone she trusts. And Arno is so likeable, you know. I mean, *I* like the kid, and I don't usually see eye-to-eye with poofters."

Jimmy chose not to reply to that comment. Trying to cure his dad of homophobia was like trying to rid the world of COVID.

But this was his chance to speak to his father about this deal.

Madeleine Muller

If not now, then when,

"Dad, I was wondering about Mrs Braithwaite. I mean, what will happen to her if she had to leave this farm? Is there not perhaps a chance one can help the reserve, after all, to save the animals and all the people working here?"

Marthinus scoffed. Luckily he seemed to be in a good mood, for instead of a biting reply, he took the time to answer,

"Ah, Jimmy. You are so young, my boy. This reserve is on its last legs. The animals are all dying and moving away, and the place is a wreck. There is no salvation. This is genuinely the best thing we can do for her. With the payout, she can buy herself a little townhouse in a retirement village. She can even take that cheetah with her. Will probably do it some good."

Jimmy felt a small prick of suspicion. This was more than just a sales job. His dad knew something that Jimmy and Mrs Braithwaite didn't. He prodded a bit further,

"But, Dad, maybe it's just been too dry or something, and once the winter is over, perhaps the place will recover."

Marthinus looked at Jimmy and then gave a quick furtive glance around the empty lounge. Jimmy felt his suspicion deepen. Marthinus' voice dropped to a whisper, "I can guarantee you, boy, there will be no recovery. And the further she and that cheetah get away from this godforsaken place, the better for both of them." He nodded knowingly, but Jimmy was even more confused than ever.

They were interrupted by Dr Kuzmich, who arrived in the lounge slightly out of breath, his forehead glistening with sweat, a few strands of hair plastered over his bald patch.

"Ah, Marthinus. We might have a problem. The Green Scorpions have gone out on a reconnaissance this morning towards the dam." Jimmy noticed Dr Kuzmich giving Jimmy a nervous look.

Mr Brandt did not seem perturbed, "Relax, my friend. They will only confirm what we already know - the utter devastation of this once beautiful reserve. This will count in our favour."

"But what if...." Dr Kuzmich licked his lips nervously, glancing in Jimmy's direction, "... if they notice something. It's just on the other side of that dam...."

But before he could finish, Mr Brandt cut him short, "Now, now. Let them notice all those poor animals, as I've said. And let them come and report back. Trust me. This is exactly what Mrs Braithwaite needs to hear."

Jimmy noticed his dad giving Dr Kuzmich a pointed look, the kind of 'we will speak of this no further here' look - and then Jimmy knew for certain that there was something his dad had not told him. Some terrible secret.

And it has something to do with those sick animals....

Madeleine Muller

Indigo

Chapter 24: *Indigo*

Indigo realised that ne were not enjoying this particular adventure. For one, it seemed as if nir skill set had no relevance in solving this dilemma, and all these sick animals were just breaking nir heart. Arno and nem had been carefully scouring the bush, geo-tagging each animal they found, and there had been loads. It seemed to be mostly mammals, no sick frogs or turtles or anything, but there was a clear lack of birds around. The only things that seemed to thrive were the insects and the cicadas, still humming loudly in the bush.

The first creatures they had found had been a family of warthogs, an adult sow and two warthog piglets, all lying closely huddled together. They were in a similar state to Nyama, and Indigo had felt slightly nauseous, remembering Bonnie and Nina's descriptions of how these animals were suffering. Indigo had no doubt that it was the same thing affecting them all.

Abongile had helped Indigo and Arno download the Green Scorpion geo-location app - and it was quick to take pictures of the family of warthogs and pin their location with a tag. They didn't say anything, but Indigo could see the distress on Arno's face. He was a sensitive boy, and ne put a hand on his shoulder. Arno was almost as tall as nem, and when he looked back at nem, eye-to-eye, and smiled, Indigo realised that ne had found another friend.

Always a loner, and now suddenly a whole crowd of new people around nem.

Soon after, they spotted a small group of Impala. Still standing but trembling, the animals only moved a couple of metres away when the youths stumbled upon them. Usually, the buck would be bolting upon their arrival.

"Sitting ducks," Arno said.

But Indigo disagreed when they found a dead jennet, already decomposing, "I don't think so. The predators are as sick as the prey. Nothing is being hunted, and nothing is doing the hunting."

Ne felt close to tears. It all felt so hopeless. By the time they had returned to the rest of the group, Indigo felt ready to go home.

What was the point?

Ne had always been aware of the horror of climate change and the devastation of human civilisation on nature, but ne didn't think ne could watch a whole ecosystem actually dying. It felt like scene in a post-apocalyptic movie. And there was nothing ne could do.

They found the group of children quiet and pensive. Nina looked pale and exhausted, with the shrub hare lying quietly on her lap.

"Ag shame, is it dead?" Arno asked, and Indigo wanted to quiet him; ne didn't even want to hear the answer. Enough now!

But Nina shook her head, "No. He is in a special sleep. Not suffering. He is not getting better, but he is also not getting worse, so that is good. You found some more, didn't you?"

Indigo was puzzled by the answer but, instead of replying, filled them in briefly on all the animals they had tagged. Not long after that, they were joined by Abongile and Alex, with descriptions of ill buck and a troop of disoriented and apathetic velvet monkeys.

Indigo kept staring at the not-dead shrub hare - it didn't look like it was breathing, and yet it did not look like a dead animal. It was the strangest thing. Ne carefully studied the children.

Something was up. Ne looked at Tess.

Madeleine Muller

"Ok then, Tess. What is the plan? It is clear you guys have been hatching something. And it's fine if we are not allowed to know what it is - just give us something to do to help."

Indigo understood that sometimes you led the mission, and sometimes you just had to follow instructions. Up to now ne had always been the leader in nir missions, but this time it was time to step back - as long as ne could just be kept busy.

Indigo had thought Tess would be taking charge as usual, but this time the little girl just stared back at Indigo in shock. She looked worried and distressed. An uncomfortable silence followed.

Abongile said, "I don't understand what's going on."

It was Bonnie who spoke.

"Ok. This is going to be difficult to explain but please just go with it. Mila can help these animals to get some temporary reprieve - she has just done that for this shrub hare. Please don't ask us how. It doesn't really matter. We can't cure them, and we don't know why they are sick. But it will win us some time. We want to try and help each and every animal for as big a radius as we can manage to cover. The geolocation will really help, as it means Nina does not have to help find all these animals."

Mila added, "We are uncomfortable with how much Nina is affected every time she tunes in…."

Alex nodded in agreement, "Nina, maybe you should go home to rest, and we will take it from here. If Mila is able to help in some way, then you can have a break…." but Nina shook her head vigorously.

"No, Alex. The bush is really thick. You will never find all the animals. I don't have to tune in to each one, but I will be able to find ones that are hidden away. We must help as many as we can. Please."

Indigo looked carefully at Nina. She looked thin, and her eyes were haunted and dull. Indigo agreed that this was taking too much of a toll, but even though Nina looked exhausted, her lips were set in a line of determination. No one was going to convince her to not try and save every animal she could.

"Ok, then," Indigo said, "while you lot go around doing your magic, we better figure out what the hell is going on. It is clear that this sound is permeating everywhere. It's affecting the animals and possibly the birds, and at the moment, we think it is man-made. What we don't know is where it is coming from. Abongile, what do you think?"

Abongile jumped on this question with enthusiasm. Indigo felt sorry for the large ranger. Having a strange bunch of kids doing all these very odd things had him completely overwhelmed. Like Indigo, he needed a clear direction.

"Good thinking, Indigo. The sooner we solve this mystery, the better. I think it would be good to update Mrs Braithwaite and Mr Dyani and let them know our suspicions. Perhaps they can help us figure out if there is some machine or something that is producing this so-called noise."

Inwardly Indigo sighed.

So Abongile was not completely convinced about the sound Nina was hearing, but at least he seemed willing to go with it for now.

It was decided that Indigo and Arno would return with Alex and Abongile and start their investigations back at the main office. Nina, Bonnie, Mila, Tess and Ryan would continue to look for animals and do their thing. Indigo looked again at the shrub hare. In the car, the girls had mentioned their powers. Ne knew Bonnie was a telepath and Mila had some weird power over time, but ne wasn't sure what Mila had done.

But ne didn't quibble. You don't ask why - you just get the job done. And this problem was far from solved.

As ne followed Abongile, Alex and Arno to the car, Mila caught up with nem.

"Hey, Indigo."

Indigo turned round, and nir heart gave a little leap. Mila always seemed more present than everyone else - like she was the queen and this was her domain. Today her usual "devil-may-care" attitude was gone - she seemed all business, her green eyes filled with purpose. She wore a pair of skin-tight jeans and a tight-fitting black t-shirt with '*Born to Roll the Rock*' printed on it.

"It will be dark in a few hours, and I don't think Nina should be doing this for too long. Will you come pick us up at about 6.00 p.m.?"

Indigo nodded, "Can I not bring you guys some food or something. You going to be ok?"

Mila smiled, "Don't worry. Tess has probably packed supplies for two days." She dropped her voice, "But I am worried about Nina."

Indigo agreed, "Can you not help her like you are helping these animals? The shrub hare seems very peaceful."

Mila sighed, "Unfortunately, that will take Nina out of the game. I am crafting a time bubble around each animal - freezing them in a moment of time. It means that for the time being, they don't suffer and they don't sicken further, but they are not good for anything else. We need Nina."

Indigo looked past where Nina and Bonnie were sitting. They were busy placing the shrub hare in a nest made of soft grass.

"Ask Bonnie to keep an eye on the situation," Indigo said, concerned, "There might come a point where you don't have a choice but to do the same for her. I don't think it is a good idea if she gets too ill. She might not recover - unless any of you have magic healing powers."

Indigo noticed Mila shiver, and the twin's gaze darkened, "Don't worry. There was this time once when I intervened too late. A friend of ours, Dawie, almost died.[55] I won't make that mistake again."

Indigo smiled sympathetically, "You carry a heavy burden, don't you, Mila? Of all of us, you have the most power and the most responsibility. You do it well."

Mila made eye contact, and a look of understanding passed between Mila and nem.

Mila said, "I am glad you are here, Indigo. It feels good to have a third pillar - it gives us strength."

Indigo gave a little laugh, "I thought you had Tess."

Mila smiled, "Shame, man. Tess is just a kid. She's the person in the chair, the sidekick. She likes to think she is in charge, but I would never put her in harm's way. But you on the other hand...."

Indigo felt nemself straighten. Mila trusted and relied on nem. Ne only nodded in reply. Nothing more needed to be said.

"I'll see you at 6.00 p.m. Let me know if you need me to come earlier."

---

[55] See 'Runnin' on the Flats'

Superheroes in Sterkstroom

Mila gave nir a winning smile and headed back to start her mission. She was wearing a big pair of solid khaki hiking boots and strode across the veldt with confident long strides.

If this were a movie, she would be walking in slow motion, Indigo thought and felt nemself flush. What was ne thinking? Mila had a boyfriend. Some Indian guy in Durban. Ne had no time for this nonsense.

Stay focused, man. Stay focused.

Madeleine Muller

Arno

Chapter 25: *Arno*

As soon as Abongile dropped Arno off in front of his rondawel, his phone started pinging with messages as he picked up signal. Mostly from Jimmy. The first messages were all relaxed,

'Hey bro, where are you?'

But the last one had a sense of urgency, "Call me! ASAP!"

Arno didn't bother to reply but quickly headed indoors. Jimmy was there, walking up and down from one side of the room to the other, shaking his hands nervously up and down - a classic Jimmy in a panic.

"Hey, sweetie. You ok?" but Arno could see that Jimmy was clearly not ok.

Arno stopped Jimmy in his tracks by putting his hand on his shoulder, and unexpectedly Jimmy flung himself into Arno's arms, burying his head in his shoulder. He was shaking, and Arno wondered if he was crying. Arno felt his heart lurch. How to comfort his friend without it getting weird…

Tentatively, he held Jimmy close, putting his one hand on his head, like you would for a child. It felt slightly odd; the two of them were almost exactly the same height. Arno felt Jimmy's frame shake.

Ok, so he was definitely crying.

Arno didn't say anything, and the two of them just stood there. Jimmy was warm and close in his arms, sobbing into his shirt.

Superheroes in Sterkstroom

Just go with it, Arno thought. *Take these moments when they come.*

After a few minutes, Jimmy calmed down and pulled away. Arno was relieved to see that his friend seemed unembarrassed, tears still streaked across his cheeks. Arno took Jimmy's hand and led him to the edge of the bed to sit down. He squeezed in next to him, still holding his hand and looked at him carefully.

What was going on?

Jimmy took a deep, shuddering breath.

"Sorry. I did not expect to start crying. It's been a rough day."

Arno just nodded, suddenly feeling guilty for spending the day out in the veldt on a big adventure. He had hardly given Jimmy a thought.

"What happened?"

Jimmy shrugged, "It's not so much one thing. It's like this final realisation. Something I've always known but never really admitted."

Arno swallowed nervously. Surely not?

"It's my dad."

Arno let out a small sigh.

Of course it would be about Jimmy's dad.

"What about him?" Arno asked, feeling on more familiar ground.

"He is a bad, bad man, Arno. I'm the son of one of those evil monsters. And not even a cool one, just a pathetic one."

Arno nodded sympathetically. This was not exactly news, but perhaps Jimmy had never seen it clearly till now.

"And what has the evil bastard done now?" Arno asked.

"I don't know," Jimmy said, "But I think him and Mr Kuzmich have got something to do with all these animals getting sick and everything. Maybe they are poisoning the water… Actually, I have no idea how they did it, but there is definitely something going on."

Arno was momentarily stunned. All the pieces were suddenly falling into place.

"I have some idea of what they might be up to," he said, his mind whirling.

Jimmy looked at Arno in surprise and pulled his hand away in horror, "What do you mean? Don't tell me you knew about all of this?" The hurt and anger in Jimmy's voice caught Arno off guard, and suddenly he felt his own tears welling up. Why were things always so difficult around Jimmy?

"No, no! It was something I discovered only this afternoon. When I went on that game drive. We… We found something," Arno worried about how to explain. He had been let into Bonnie, Mila and Nina's closely guarded secrets. It didn't seem right to share them, not even with Jimmy. But he needed to say something and opted for a small white lie.

"Abongile has figured out what is causing the problem with all those sick animals. It's not the water. It is some weird high-pitched noise that only animals can hear. They think that it is man-made, maybe some machine malfunctioning somewhere. But this would make sense. If Dr Kuzmich and your father had managed to create some device that produced a sound that could clear the nature reserve of most of its animals…."

"But that is terrible!" Jimmy wailed. "Like worse than terrible!"

Arno had to agree. But didn't really want to say so.

"But we can't say for sure yet, Jimmy. I mean, it's just a theory. What if we are just picking up *stompies*[56] here like?"

Jimmy stood up and started pacing back and forth again. For a moment, Arno felt bereft of his friend's presence so close to him. Jimmy was rambling,

"We can't just accuse my dad. He will deny everything. And if we go to the police, we have no proof. And if we did have evidence, my dad would be in so much trouble. I mean, he could even go to jail or something."

Arno interjected, "We have to tell Abongile…."

"No!" Jimmy stopped him mid-track, "I can't just throw my dad under the bus. We don't even know if it's true."

Arno lowered his voice, hoping to calm Jimmy down a bit, "Yeah, but what about the animals, Jimmy? They are suffering terribly, and many of them are dying. We got to stop that noise."

Jimmy stood in the middle of the room like a rabbit caught in the headlights. Arno could see him wracking his brains, trying to find a way

---

[56] cigarette butts. An Afrikaans saying - making assumptions

out. Arno waited. This was Jimmy's dad, Jimmy's life. Jimmy needed to decide what to do.

After a minute, Jimmy looked up, "Dr Kuzmich had said something about the dam. On the other side. He was worried that Abongile was going to find something there. We need to go and look and figure it out before the Green Scorpions do."

Arno's forehead broke out in a cold sweat. That's where all those kids were poking around, looking for sick animals. It would be so much easier if he could just tell them what was going on. But his first loyalty was to Jimmy. He had to find a way to stop that noise but at the same time protect Jimmy, which meant keeping Mr Brandt out of this for now. Slowly a plan was forming.

"Ok, Jimmy. I've got an idea. I can down to the dam this evening. Legato can take me. The kids are all tracking the sick animals with this cool geo-tracking app, which means I can tell where they are and make sure not to bump into them. I will go and check out the dam and see if I can find the problem."

"You mean *we* will go," Jimmy corrected him, but Arno was already shaking his head.

"That's just stupid. You are supposed to meet your dad for supper, remember. And if we both get caught snooping around, we are screwed. You need to stay here and keep an eye on your dad and Dr Kuzmich."

Arno stood up, walked over to Jimmy and stood in front of him. "Or who is going to come and rescue me, hey?"

Jimmy's eyes widened.

"Don't worry, darling. Just jokes. It will be easy peasy pudding and pie. But I need you here, ok?"

Jimmy sighed but nodded, "Ok, Arno. But keep Lerato with you, please, man."

Arno frowned, "Ja, hey. Not sure what I am going to tell *Tata*," and then, with a cheeky smile, "but the old man has never been able to say no to me."

Madeleine Muller

Chapter 26: *Bonnie*

The five kids spent the rest of the afternoon locating animals with Mila 'doing her magic,' as Tess put it. Bonnie looked at the group with concern. The only one who seemed to be thriving was Mila. She always became stronger when she was using her powers, and each 'freezing' was going faster and faster. They had worked out an efficient system of Ryan and Tess scouting ahead and finding what animals they could. Nina followed after, locating animals that Ryan and Tess might have missed. Bonnie hovered around Nina, keeping an eye on her. They pinned locations on the app, and Mila followed to freeze each animal in turn.

But Ryan and Tess were definitely starting to flag. Bonnie could tell it was more the emotional drain of it all than the physical effort of walking through the thick bush. They both loved animals, and each suffering creature touched them deeply.

But she was most worried about Nina. The little girl was trying to put on a brave face, but Bonnie did not even have to tune in to see the child was exhausted. Every now and then, Bonnie would do a proper check and was shocked at how ill Nina was actually feeling. She was exhausted and nauseous, and extraordinarily thirsty. Luckily, Tess had brought tonnes of water bottles, but with all the drinking, Nina kept on having to pop behind strategic bushes, and Tess was getting worried they would run out of loo paper.

Superheroes in Sterkstroom

Mila had warned Bonnie to let her know when things were getting out of hand, but Bonnie didn't know how to tell. Perhaps they should have turned back hours ago? What if she was making the wrong call to let Nina continue?

Mila caught up with her twin and seemed to be reading Bonnie's mind. She whispered in her sister's ear, "I don't think Nina would let you stop her. Don't worry. Indigo has just sent a message and is on their way to pick us up. A good night's rest is all she needs."

Bonnie nodded but was suddenly not so sure.

What if something were to happen to Nina on her watch? She shuddered at the thought.

Madeleine Muller

Indigo

Chapter 27: *Indigo*

Indigo, Abongile and Alex were sitting in Mrs Braithwaite's sitting room. Mrs Braithwaite had insisted on making the tea, but Indigo noticed that Mr Dyani helped her to carry in the tray with an old-fashioned teapot and cups and saucers. She was frailer than she let on.

"How is Nyama?" Alex asked, "I'm still waiting for the blood results, so I don't have much news yet, I'm afraid."

"Oh, very much the same," Mrs Braithwaite answered. "Thank you so much for trying to help, but I am starting to give up hope."

Indigo's heart lurched. It would be great if Mila could also give Nyama a bit of respite, but how to explain that to Mrs Braithwaite?

Abongile cleared his throat, "Mrs Braithwaite, we did a bit of investigating this morning, and we have a new theory. About the ill animals…." Abongile hesitated, and Alex took over,

"It might be that the problem is not pollution but to do with a sound."

"Sound?" Mr Dyani sat up, "What do you mean?"

Alex was looking uncomfortable, and Indigo realised that Abongile and her had not really bought into the story quite yet. Time to step in.

"I am studying physics, Mrs Braithwaite," Indigo started. Well, it was sort of true. Ne was planning to do a degree in physics. Eventually.

"And we have picked up a high-pitched, distorted sound. A noise only animals can hear. We are not sure if this is causing the problem, but just to give an example, have you ever experienced a really annoying sound…?"

"Like a car alarm?" Mr Dyani suggested.

"Exactly. And imagine you are trying to sleep, and this car alarm goes off somewhere, and it just goes on and on… In the end, it would drive you nuts. Well, if there were a disruptive sound going on for days or weeks on end in the nature reserve, that could be very disturbing to the animals. It would disrupt their routines, their ability to feed, their migration, and their mating rituals. And the animals wouldn't be able to get away from it. It would be there twenty-four hours a day."

Mrs Braithwaite looked puzzled, "You mean Nyama is hearing this noise? But we can't hear anything?"

Mr Dyani turned to the old lady. He was quicker on the uptake. "It's like a dog whistle, Abigail. Only the animals can hear it. It would explain why the environmentalists who came and tested the dam water did not find anything. You can't test for noise." Then he turned to Indigo, who had managed to impress him with nir confidence.

"And what could be making this noise?"

"We don't know," Indigo admitted. "It might be some malfunctioning machinery. As we can't measure or hear it, it is difficult to determine its location. We hoped you might have some ideas."

"A machine…?" Mrs Braithwaite said, and Indigo could see that this conversation was too much for her. Mr Dyani patted her kindly on the knee.

"Don't worry, Abigail. This is just a theory. But I will help the Green Scorpions to look into it," and then turning back to Abongile,

"Give me some time to think about this. I will dig out the map of Mpangwa with all the buildings on and around it. Then we can identify any potential sources. I will bring it to the dining room at breakfast. In some ways, this would be good news. If we could find the cause of all this misery…."

"Don't get your hopes up, Mr Dyani," Alex said, "It is a bit of a long shot."

But Indigo thought that a long shot was exactly what they needed.

Chapter 28: *Nina*

Nina allowed herself to be tucked under the covers. It was only 7.00 p.m., but she had passed out in the car on the way home, and Bonnie had insisted she go straight to bed. Tess had organised her a quick toasted sandwich from the bar, and she had wolfed it down hungrily. She could easily have eaten several but didn't want to bother Tess. Nina closed her eyes. She was exhausted but was not sure she could sleep. Although she couldn't actually hear that noise at the moment, she could imagine it humming in the background.

"Perhaps we should put her in a bubble, Mila?" Nina heard Bonnie's question from far away and felt vaguely puzzled by it.

What bubble?

"Not a good idea," Mila said. "She needs to actually sleep. And for her body to refresh and repair, she needs *time* asleep. A time bubble will just freeze her in the moment, and she will come out of it as exhausted as ever."

"Of course," Bonnie replied. "I am not thinking straight."

Nina opened her eyes.

"Bonnie. Don't worry. I'll be ok. We did good work today. Tomorrow we need to keep going. As soon as we get up. Please. I cannot bear the idea of animals being tortured by that horrible noise."

Bonnie gave her a reassuring smile, "Sure. But we are going to stop and come back for regular breaks. We cannot keep going at the same intensity as today. Deal?

"Deal," Nina said. "I'm really glad you guys are here. We couldn't have done this without you."

Mila went and sat down on the other side of the bed, gently stroking Nina's hair, "No problem, kiddo. We're your team, remember."

Nina let herself drift off to sleep - ignoring the aching, the nausea, and the thirst. No matter what was going on out there, she felt safe here amongst her friends.

With friends like these watching over her, surely everything would be ok.

Madeleine Muller

Chapter 29: *Arno*

Arno flicked on his head torch. It was already close to 8.00 p.m., and as soon as the sun had dipped under the horizon, they had been dunked in darkness. No moon out yet. He passed a hand-held torch to Lerato, who switched it on gingerly. The old man had been surprisingly keen to help. Jimmy and Arno had explained about the noise the Green Scorpions had 'detected' but had blamed its possible source on Dr Kuzmich. Arno guessed that Lerato would hate to feel he was being disloyal to Mr Brandt and decided to leave out his father's possible involvement. He felt a bit guilty about the lie.

But he couldn't drive, and there had been no other way of getting to the dam. You sure as hell couldn't walk through the bush at night - you might get trampled by a rhino or something.

Lerato had carefully navigated the Mercedes down the dusty road, muttering under his breath. It had been a different route than the one Abongile had followed earlier that day - a fairly well-graded track that took tourists to a lookout point over the dam. Arno had hoped it would get them close enough. Once they had arrived at the parking lot, and against Jimmy's advice, Arno had tried to convince Lerato to stay in the car, but the old man would have none of it.

"Mr Brandt would not approve if I let you blunder off on your own in the bush at night. I am coming."

Superheroes in Sterkstroom

Always practical, Lerato had dressed in the long-sleeved navy overalls and a solid pair of gumboots he reserved for when he checked under the precious Merc for leaks. Arno thought Lerato looked like a miner on one of those Anglo-American posters, but he, himself, had struggled to find an appropriate outfit. Dark jeans seemed sensible, but most of his shirts were billowy and bright. The best he could do was a muted baby-blue blouse, and Jimmy had lent him a black hoody to wear over it. Combined with his most sensible pair of *tekkies*, Arno felt positively dull. The only concession to style he made was tying up his hair into two half-ponies on top of his head, ostensibly to be able to fit the head torch over his forehead.

As they made their way down the track towards the dam, Arno wondered if they shouldn't have waited till morning. There was no moon out yet. It was so damn dark you could only see a few metres ahead; the only light came from their flimsy torches. How on earth were they going to find anything?

They reached the dam and turned down a track leading to the right. Jimmy had said that Dr Kuzmich had mentioned the "back" of the dam.

Arno checked his phone again.

There was no MTN signal, but Arno did have a satellite connection to the geo-tagging app. The kids had not mapped any animals since 6.00 p.m., and he assumed they were all safely back home. Just before he and Lerato had left, Jimmy had confirmed that Mr Brandt and Dr Kuzmich were at dinner, and knowing old Marthinus, they would probably be drinking *Klippies and coke*[57] till late. The bastard would not be too pleased that Arno had not made an appearance to woo Mrs Braithwaite.

Ag well. Tough titties.

"Arno, *mtwana'm*[58]. What is the plan here?" Lerato asked, and Arno was surprised by the authority in the old man's voice. He certainly was not the quiet chauffeur Arno usually regaled with all his stories.

"You seem all happy in the bush, Tata?" Arno commented, a smile in his voice. "You from rural, *baba*[59]?"

---

[57] Klipdrift (a whiskey) and coke
[58] my child (isiXhosa)
[59] father (respectful)

"My home is not far from here," Lerato replied, "I grew up in a village, *ndawoni*[60] Cofimvaba. I guess you boys from the Flats will call that 'deep rural'. I spent many nights in the bush with our cattle when I was a child."

"You miss it," Arno said matter of factly.

"*Ewe*[61]. I loved being out at night, looking up at all those stars. You don't see the stars in Cape Town. Not like here."

Arno had reached a point where the path veered away from the dam and had to make a decision. He suspected that whatever was causing that sound would surely be tucked out of sight.

"I'm not even sure what we are looking for. Are you up to some bundu bashing, Tata? We are going to turn off the path here."

Lerato grunted, "I should have brought my panga…" but gamely followed Arno through the long grass, ducking under the overhanging branches. The light from the head torch threw eery shadows over the trees and veldt, and Arno shivered, even though he was sweating from walking. What he needed was some supercool superpower to help find this thing they were looking for. It was all starting to feel a bit foolish.…

What had he been thinking?

Suddenly Lerato grabbed him by his backpack, bringing him to a halt. Arno almost screamed in fright.

"*Thula,*"[62] Lerato said.

Arno did as he was told, and they both stood in the bush, listening to the night noises. Arno looked back at Lerato and shrugged his shoulders in a silent question. Lerato put his finger to his mouth, and then Arno heard it.

Voices.

It was quite far away, but there was the low grumbling of men talking. Lerato squeezed past Arno and gestured to him to switch off his torch. Arno did so, albeit with some reservation. Lerato kept his light on, pointing straight down and headed off in a semi-crouch. Arno was

---

[60] nearby
[61] Yes
[62] Quiet

impressed by how quietly the old man moved. Lerato would give Nyama a go with his soft padded gait.

The voices became louder, and suddenly Arno was immensely grateful for having Lerato there. No way would he have been able to pinpoint the direction of the sound. Lerato switched off his light completely, and Arno realised they must be getting close. The old man walked another few metres, then hunched down and pulled away some branches.

And there they were.

Two men, one of them holding a lantern. They were dressed in security guard uniforms with black batons and guns in holsters on their belts.

So not ordinary security guards, then.

The guards were smoking, occasionally conversing in low voices in isiXhosa, but Arno couldn't hear. Arno's whispered to Lerato.

"Can you hear what they are saying?"

Lerato shrugged and whispered back, "Nothing of importance. Just chit-chat. But I think they are guarding something behind them."

Arno squinted his eyes. The lantern the security guard was holding did not provide much light, and the two men seemed to be standing in some random dense bush. But when Arno looked carefully, he could see what Lerato was referring to. There was a small concrete structure, maybe of a reservoir or something, a couple of metres beyond the chatting men. He could just make out the low curved concrete wall, but not much else.

Why would someone be guarding some ancient-looking reservoir?

Very suspicious.

This had to be what Dr Kuzmich was referring to.

Lerato tapped Arno on the shoulder and mouthed, "*Masihambe*....[63]"

Arno was inclined to agree. No point in going any closer tonight. They would have to come back in the morning. But how on earth would he find this place tomorrow?

---

[63] Let us go (isiXhosa)

Madeleine Muller

Quickly he took out his phone and, hunching over to block the light from the screen, he pinned his location on the geo-location app and added a label:

> Reservoir

He wasn't sure how he was going to explain all this to the others, so best to keep it neutral for now. He would just have to come back in the morning and figure it out.

Arno put his phone in his pocket, and Lerato gave him a questioning look that was only just visible in the pitch dark. Arno gave him a thumbs up and gestured for him to lead the way. He had geo-tagged the parking lot where they had left the car, but it was best not to start tracking the route back yet until they were well away from those two guys.

But Lerato did not hesitate and easily found his way through the veldt. Arno was impressed. He had completely lost any sense of direction. When they got back to the track, Lerato switched on his torch, and Arno let out a sigh of relief. So far, so good.

But then, unexpectedly, a deep voice in the dark made Arno jump.

"*Wie's daar*[64]?"

The man switched on a flashlight and shone it straight into Arno and Lerato's eyes. He couldn't see a thing.

Arno thought quickly, "*Naand, Oom*.[65] Yho. You gave us a fright, hey. We were checking out the game at the dam at sunset but got ourselves a bit lost, like. But it's fine. We found the track now."

Arno suddenly regretted the two half-ponies with their rainbow-coloured hair ties. Not exactly a game-watcher's look.

"*Moenie kak praat nie*.[66] I saw you creeping through the bush, all secretive. You are coming with me now."

Arno looked at Lerato, who imperceptibly shook his head.

---

[64] Who is there?
[65] Good evening, uncle
[66] Don't talk nonsense

Superheroes in Sterkstroom

"No, we'd rather not, Oom. We've got Abongile waiting for us in the parking lot."

If the man had seen them skulking around, it might be best to align himself with the cops.

But the man just laughed and continued in a heavy Afrikaans accent, "I've just been up there, and there is no one waiting, *jou klein snert*.[67] Now bring that boy of yours and come."

Arno felt his anger rise. He could take insults all day, but disrespect to your elders would not be tolerated. But Lerato must have seen what was coming and quietly grabbed Arno's arm.

"*Unompu…*[68]" Arno squinted into the light and then noticed the revolver in the man's hand, his arm hanging down relaxed at the side, but the finger on the trigger nevertheless.

"Oh, kak," Arno said and turned to Lerato,

"*Uxolo Baba,*[69]" I didn't mean for you to get involved in this."

"No, Arno, it's not your fault," Lerato said, "You are not the one with a gun."

---

[67] You little trouble-maker

[68] He has a gun

[69] I'm sorry father

Madeleine Muller

Jimmy

Chapter 30: *Jimmy*

Jimmy shuffled around on his chair. They were still in the dining room, and he had long finished his food, but it was essential he stayed and made sure his dad and Dr Kuzmich did not get wind of Arno's harebrained plan. He had been sending Arno messages, but the single tick showed that none of them were going through. But Arno did say there was no signal in the bush. And Lerato was with him. So they should be fine.

Jimmy looked at his watch. It was 9.10 p.m. He would have to keep his dad distracted for at least another hour to be safe. At the moment, the two men seemed quite relaxed, drinking after dinner port and discussing the latest South Africa vs All Blacks rugby game.

The evening had not started well when Mr Brandt had discovered that Arno was 'down with flu', but since Mrs Braithwaite and Mr Dyani had not shown up for supper either, he had quickly settled down. Both men seemed confident that the deal was practically sealed, and Jimmy was starting to feel less and less sure about being able to do anything about it. Hopelessness washed over him, and he thought of Arno. Whenever he felt down, or distressed or anxious, all he had to do was imagine Arno's smile and his uproarious laugh, and he would feel better. But now, when he thought of Arno, he was drowned in waves of worry.

He should never have agreed for Arno to go.

Superheroes in Sterkstroom

Dr Kuzmich's phone rang, and the sweaty man glanced down at his phone to see who was calling. A frown furrowed his brow as he stood up. "Sorry, Marthinus, just gotta take this one."

The Russian stepped out via one of the side doors, but he was still visible on the stoep through the large glass windows of the dining room. Jimmy watched him out of the corner of his eye. Something was wrong. Dr Kuzmich was clearly furious, walking up and down while hissing into the phone. Jimmy felt himself shiver and wished he could hear what the man was saying.

Who would call this late at night?

Was this about Arno and Lerato?

When Dr Kuzmich returned, he was visibly agitated.

"Everything ok?" Marthinus Brandt asked, looking very mellow after several whiskeys. Jimmy noticed Dr Kuzmich adjusting his features, putting on a fake smile.

"No, no. Just a small problem at one of the other parks - a couple of poachers. But it is all sorted now."

Jimmy felt his heart rate go through the roof and his breathing struggling to keep up. Why was Dr Kuzmich so clearly lying to his dad? Surely if they caught Arno and Lerato, he would tell him? Unless he had planned something that Mr Brandt wouldn't approve of.

Jimmy stood up, almost knocking over the chair.

"I have to go," he said, barely getting the words out. "I am really tired."

But Dr Kuzmich took his arm in an iron clench, pulling him back down.

"Now, now, Jimmy. The evening is still young. Let me get you a proper drink, young man."

And then Jimmy knew for sure. Arno had been caught. And Dr Kuzmich was planning to keep him there until whatever instructions he had given had been carried out. Jimmy smiled back, relaxed his body, and as he felt Dr Kuzmich's grip loosen, he jerked his arm free and almost ran out of the dining room.

"Jimmy. What are you doing?"

Madeleine Muller

He could hear his father's voice shouting after him but did not stop to look around. Enough of this skulking around. If he had to choose between his dad and Arno, there was only one option.

Chapter 31: *Tess*

Tess was sitting in the front lounge of their three-roomed rondawel, paging through the notes in her notebook. She was sure the answer was right there. They were missing something important. What would be causing such a terribly high-pitched noise that would traumatise all these animals?

It was already after 8.00 p.m., and Nina, Bonnie and Mila were all in bed, fast asleep. Nina had fallen asleep in the car on their way back from the dam and had barely managed to eat her supper before collapsing in bed. Bonnie had looked as grey as Nina, and although Mila had seemed remarkably sprightly after putting almost a hundred different animals into little time bubbles, she had happily gone to bed when both her sisters had settled.

The rondawel was dead quiet. Indigo and Alex were not back from their visit to Mrs Braithwaite and Mr Dyani, and Arno had gone home to Jimmy. Ryan had promised to stay up and help Tess figure things out, but he was lying beside her on the couch, gently snoring.

Probably a good thing. Tess could use the time to think and figure stuff out. It felt like a puzzle with a missing piece.

What did they know, really? Only that some strange noise was upsetting the animals. What was making it.?

Perhaps there was a pattern to a disease that they had missed.

Madeleine Muller

Tess opened her iPad on her lap and clicked on the geo-tagging app. She zoomed in and aimlessly scrolled from one set of animals to the next - impala, some meerkats, a family of jennets, one lone hyena, and then something odd caught her eye.

An entry, off to the one side at the back of the dam.

$$\boxed{\text{Reservoir}}$$

Tess was confused. They hadn't even visited that part of the dam. There had been surprisingly few animals in that direction, so they had stayed close to the water's edge. Tess felt a niggle of disquiet. Maybe that *is* significant - the lack of animals....

She clicked on 'reservoir' to get more details. The time of the tagging was 8.45 p.m. Tess checked her watch - it was 8.50 p.m. now. That means someone had set the tag a mere five minutes ago. There was no other entry - no explanation or description. Tess sat back and looked at the screen in confusion. Everyone was here, weren't they? Or maybe Abongile and Alex had gone out again tonight?

Just then, the door opened, and Indigo walked in. Ryan woke up with a start, "Hey, what?"

"Howzit, Ryan. You should be in bed. And Tess. You ok? You have the frown of a small highway running between your eyebrows." Indigo seemed relaxed and in full-power mode.

Tess felt relief wash over her. As much as she liked detecting, she hated doing this kind of thing on her own. She was at her best in a team.

"There is something odd on the geotagging app," she said, "Has Abongile or Alex gone back out again tonight?"

Indigo shook nir head, "Nope. We have been pouring over some local maps that Mr Dyanti managed to find. Nothing looked very hopeful, but we were going to go and explore first thing in the morning. They are still up talking. I went past Arno's, but their rondawel was pitch dark, so I assumed he was also asleep. What's up?"

Superheroes in Sterkstroom

Tess showed Indigo and Ryan the the strange new location that had just popped up. Indigo sat down next to Tess and took over the scrolling.

"Look!" ne said, "Here is another one.:

$$\boxed{\text{Merc}}$$

Indigo clicked on the tag, "This one was tagged at 8.00 p.m. It's at that parking lot, just above the dam."

Tess' frown deepened even further, " I don't get it,"

"That's Arno, girl," Ryan said. "I'm telling you. He tol' me he and that mate of his came here in a Mercedes, C-Class and all. And driven down by a fancy-pantsy chauffeur, *nogal?*"

Indigo shrugged, "You think? We can't tell from this serial number who it is that is doing the tagging. But he *is* the only one that could possibly be out there. I wonder what he is up to?"

"Just give the bra a ring, Tess" Ryan suggested impatiently.

Tess tried to get through but had no luck. Probably no signal. Indigo shrugged, "It's probably nothing. We can ask him in the morning. I'm ready for bed."

But Tess couldn't shake the feeling that something was wrong.

"There is a way to check," Tess said. "Bonnie will be able to tell if it was him."

Indigo frowned, "From this far away? Surely she needs to be close by to tune in?"

Ryan put up his hand, and Tess rolled her eyes as Indigo gave him a nod to go ahead, "Bonnie can do long-distance tuning, my bra. When there are so few people around, and especially when everyone is sleeping, she can pick up signal from like miles away. That night of the shipwreck, she picked up those sailors freaking out like *this*,[70]" and Ryan clicked his fingers.

"You really want to wake her up?" Indigo asked, a note of scepticism in nir voice.

---

[70] See 'On the rocks at Mdumbi'

Tess gave it a moment's thought. It was always better to check. If it was nothing, Bonnie would simply go straight back to sleep. Always trust your gut, Bonnie said.

Ten minutes later, they had woken Bonnie up and led her to the lounge. Mila slept blissfully through their attempts to rouse her sister and kept snoring gently in oblivion.

Bonnie was so bleary from sleep that it took Tess several attempts to explain the problem.

"Ok, let me get this straight," Bonnie said, yawning, "You want me to check if Arno is out there doing something."

"Yes," Ryan and Tess said in unison.

"Why?" Bonnie asked. "Surely we can just ask him in the morning."

"Something is not right," Tess said, "Why did he go out so late? And why tag the Mercedes and the reservoir? And why did he not come and tell us if he was on to something?"

Bonnie looked at her sister wryly, "You have no patience, Tess. That is your problem. You always want the answers immediately."

"Please, Bonnie. Just help!" Tess was feeling annoyed. Her sisters never took her seriously. Not really.

Bonnie sighed and shook her head slightly. Then she sat up straight and closed her eyes. Tess looked at her sister attentively and felt a twinge of guilt. She wasn't being fair. Even though the twins could get grumpy, they always came through for her.

It seemed to take ages, and Tess could see the pale girl's eyes moving behind closed lids.

Suddenly, Bonnie's eyes flew open.

"Something is happening."

"What do you mean?" Indigo asked.

"It *is* Arno. Out there in the bush. But he is in trouble. Big trouble."

"What kind of trouble?" Tess asked, her heart now beating a mile a minute.

"I am not sure. He is so far away, but I can feel his panic. He is with someone. It is an older man - I think it must be that chauffeur. They are being threatened…."

Superheroes in Sterkstroom

"Close your eyes, Bonnie. Try again," Indigo urged. "You are panicking, and it's making it difficult for you to pick up the details." Bonnie nodded and said to Tess, "Wake, Mila."

Tess didn't hesitate and rushed to the bedroom to wake her sister, which unsurprisingly turned out to be a much harder task than rousing Bonnie.

When Tess finally returned to the lounge with Mila, Bonnie was pacing up and down. Looking at Mila, she said, "We need to suit up."

"You've got suits?" Indigo said, clear excitement in nir voice.

Tess smiled, "And they have recently been upgraded. Mila used to have a suit in pretty white but decided black would be better for night work."

"And it was a bitch to keep clean," Mila said, looking vaguely confused. "Can someone please fill me in before I squeeze my butt into skin-tight polymer?"

Bonnie explained, "It's Arno. He and his chauffeur went off on their own into the bush tonight. We assume on some reconnaissance mission. They parked their Mercedes at that parking lot at the dam at 8.00 p.m., where Arno tagged it, and then tagged a reservoir a few kilometres away at 8.45 p.m. But when I checked in just now, something was very wrong. Arno and his chauffeur are being frog-marched through the bush by someone. As far as I can tell, they might be heading back to that reservoir, but I am not too sure. But I know they are terrified, and whatever is happening is against their will."

Tess whispered nervously, "Maybe we should wake Abongile."

But Mila shook her head, "Tess, we are much better qualified than Abongile or Alex to figure this out. And there must be a reason Arno went off on his own like that in the first place. I vote we go and investigate. Indigo, could you give us a lift?"

Tess saw a look of annoyance pass over Indigo's face and knew that feeling. Indigo did not want to only be the driver. Mila must have picked it up as well, for she continued, "I think your skill set might be particularly useful tonight if we want to find out what is actually going on."

Bonnie headed to their room, "I'll get our suits. Tess, we will need you and Ryan to stay here and be our backup, especially as there is no signal out there. We can use the tagging app to communicate."

Tess felt herself bristle, "That is *not* fair! It was me that figured all of this out. No ways are you excluding me now."

Bonnie went over to Tess and put her hands on her shoulders, "I am not just being protective, Tess. We don't know what is going on at the moment. I need someone to look after Nina and, if things go wrong, someone who can explain all this to Abongile."

Bonnie paused a moment, and Tess felt a cold shiver run down her spine as her sister continued, "Nina is getting sicker, Tess. Something is not right, and I am worried. I didn't want to alarm you and hope a good night's rest might sort her out, but every time I tune into her, it just feels like it is getting worse. I want you to check on her, and if anything happens, I want you to call an ambulance. Ok?"

Tess nodded mutely. This was not a game.

Ryan stepped up beside her, "No worries, Bonnie. But clock in regularly like."

"Sure," Bonnie said, "Can't do this without you guys."

Chapter 32: *Indigo*

Indigo parked the car a few hundred metres from the parking lot and tried to hide it off road as best as ne could. It was already close to 10.00 p.m. Adrenalin was coursing through nir veins, and the night had taken on that strange, surreal feel. What made it even more surreal was that the twins, who were pretty exotic on a normal day, took it to a new level with their awesome, CSIR-designed suits. The suits consisted of pitch-black skin-tight trousers, zipped-up long-sleeved fitted shirts and calf-high boots. The material was made of Mopani worm African silk, bonded with some strange polymer, and was smooth, flexible, and tough. A sleeveless waistcoat with pockets, straps and rings ensured that they could easily load a variety of supplies.

Indigo had carefully checked but noted no obvious weapons. Ne wasn't sure if this was a good or a bad thing....

When, less than an hour ago, Mila had stepped out of the bedroom, still adjusting the fit of the top, Indigo had struggled to suppress a gasp. Mila had looked older and taller with the build of an Amazon Warrior who had the attitude of Tank Girl. Mila must have noticed nir eyes widen, for she gave Indigo a lop-sided grin,

"If you ask nicely, we'll get you one as well."

Madeleine Muller

Indigo grinned back, "No worries; if I need one, I can just shift my own...."

*

Getting out of the car without making a sound was tricky. The night was eerily quiet, and Bonnie had picked up that someone was up ahead. Indigo did not dare to lock the car, for the high tweet of the immobiliser would be a dead giveaway.

The moon was not out yet, and it was pitch dark. Mila had a small light on the strap of her watch, palm side, which she used to light a metre or so ahead. Quickly they headed up the road around the bend towards the parking lot, slowing down as they got closer. Bonnie stopped them and whispered, "Yip, someone's there."

Mila switched off her light, and they ducked through the veldt instead, crouching low a few metres from the parking lot, the Mercedes the only vehicle there. Beside it stood two men in guard uniform, talking in quiet but urgent voices. They both looked nervous, hotly debating some issue.

"Can you hear what they are saying?" Mila asked Bonnie as they crawled closer. They were on their stomachs, with Indigo in the middle and Mila's legs pressed against nir.

Bonnie shook her head, "They are talking in isiXhosa and have quite heavy accents - too hard for me to decipher. Dr Kuzmich's name came up, though. I think these guys were sent to fetch the car."

And right then, Indigo understood.

This was it.

This was nir moment.

"I've got this," was all ne said before ne shifted.

Indigo had been shifting since ne was fourteen, but it was a strange rush every time. Ne created a picture of whomever ne wanted to shift into in nir head, and slowly that picture took over and when ne opened nir eyes, ne was someone else. Indigo had to have someone specifically in mind, but in shift form, ne never looked exactly like that person. Ne would inherit their language, accent, and some personality traits but could adjust details like clothes and hairstyles.

Superheroes in Sterkstroom

It was not difficult to decide who to use as a 'pattern' for this job. Abongile came easily to mind, and Indigo could feel nemself pushing against Bonnie and Mila on either side as nir body expanded in size and bulk. In nir mind, ne removed the beard and tried to get the uniform as close as ne could to the ones the guards were wearing.

When ne opened nir eyes, ne was looking straight into Mila's eyes, wide with admiration, "Wow, dude. That is the most legit thing I have ever seen."

"Is the uniform ok?" Indigo whispered.

"There is an extra stripe on the epaulette," Mila pointed out matter-of-factly. "I know this security company."

Indigo loved how Mila just took nir shift in her stride. Ne adjusted the uniform as per Mila's instructions.
Bonnie was less sure, "I don't know if this is such a good idea. This could be really dangerous."

Indigo turned to Bonnie and said, "I want you to read my mind. I am going to say something. Can you do that?"

Bonnie nodded, looking confused. After a moment, she said, "You asked if I could hear you?"

"Good," Indigo said, "I was speaking in isiXhosa. Or at least I think I was, but when I hear it in my head, it is in English. It means you will be able to understand what's going on when I am interrogating the guards. If things get out of hand…."

"Got your back, sweetheart," Mila completed nir sentence, grinning, and Indigo grinned back before ducking back through the bush and approaching the parking lot via the road.

The two guards looked up in fright as ne approached, and Indigo put nir hands up to show all was well.

"**Good evening. Are you from Bushguard Security**?" Indigo asked. Ne knew that ne was speaking IsiXhosa, but in nir head, ne would hear the entire conversation in English. Indigo had always found this annoying. Once ne shifted back, there would be no retention of the language. As a result, nir actual IsiXhosa was pretty poor.

Both security guards were young, thin and gangly with shaven heads and faces, but the one, about a head taller than the other, stepped forward.

"*Good evening. Yes, my friend. And who are you?*"

"I am Zola," Indigo said, using nir favourite isiXhosa name, "*Dr Kuzmich asked the boss to send someone and I was in the taxi not too far past Mpangwa....*" Best to keep it vague. "*They dropped me down the road and said I should meet you here..*"

The short one now chipped in eagerly, "*Are you coming to get the car?*" And then to his tall colleague, "*This is better, Dumisa. I don't want anything to do with this nonsense.*"

"*Shut up, Madoda. We get paid well for this job. I am not letting some new guy muscle in here.*"

"*We don't get paid that well,*" Madoda, the short one, snorted, and Indigo interrupted before the argument got out of hand,

"*Hayi. I don't know anything my brothers. I was just sent to help. Nice wheels though. So who are we nicking this car for then*"

Madoda put his hands in the air, and his voice went up a notch, "*We are not stealing anything! We are just following orders. I didn't join a security company to end up being part of this rubbish.*"

Dumisa shook his head sadly, "*And who do you think is rich enough to hire security companies for details like this? They are all crooks I'm telling you. Crooks or corrupt government officials. But looks like Zola here is not too worried.*"

Indigo let out a quiet sigh of relief. Dumisa thinks has found an ally. Good.

Dumisa walked up to Indigo and put a hand on nir shoulder, "*It's nothing too bad. We are just picking up this car here and driving it up the road to meet Mr Nel and a couple of poachers they've caught. Look, we've got the keys and everything.*"

"*Poachers?*" Indigo asked.

Madoda said, "*It sounds fishy to me. I know Dr Kuzmich works for the National Parks board, but he has never given a damn about any of these animals and now he is hiring extra guys to sort out poachers? No man. It's got something to do with that bunker we are guarding*"

"*Bunker?*" Indigo asked nonchalantly. This had been easier than ne thought.

Dumisani stopped Madoda from replying, "*Hayi, Madoda. We don't know nothing, ok. They just have some high tech, expensive equipment they are storing there, that's all. Our job is to guard it, and tonight we are just helping with these poachers like good citizens. Stop overthinking it..*"

"*How many poachers,?*" Indigo risked. Ne didn't want to seem too nosy, but this seemed a reasonable question to ask.

"*Just a couple,*" Dumisani replied, walking back towards the car. He was clearly keen to get going.

"*They don't look like poachers to me,*" Madoda grumbled. "*A young coloured kid with blerrie ponytails on the top of his head and an old man. And I didn't see any guns, or any poached animals for that matter.*"

"*Oh shut up Madoda,*" Dumisani said. "*Let us go. I'm driving. Zola, why don't you get in the front. Then Madoda can do his complaining away from my ears. I am tired now.*"

Indigo only hesitated for a second. The point was to get information, but this was too good an opportunity to pass by. They would take nem straight to 'the poachers' who were clearly Arno and his chauffeur.

Ne headed for the passenger door, but suddenly, something bizarre happened.

Mila appeared out of nowhere, her hand on Indigo's arm.

Indigo almost screamed in fright and swivelled nir head towards the two other guards in panic. What was Mila thinking? Ne could not protect her if these guys pulled out guns.

And then ne noticed several things at once.

The deathly silence, the unmoving air. And the two guards, frozen in mid-step. Madoda had his head down and was suspended in mid-mutter. Dumisani had just unlocked the car with the remote key, reaching for the door.

Time.

Mila had stopped time.

Mila didn't explain. She just stood there and waited for Indigo to take it all in. Indigo liked that. It was like when ne shifted. No need to warn or say anything. Indigo smiled and took a deep breath. Ne was suddenly aware of nir beating heart and realised how completely wired ne had been during the conversation with the guards.

But now there was … time.

"Good work," Mila said, "Sorry to have given you a fright but always good to have a plan."

"Fair enough," Indigo said, shifting nir thoughts back to English, still looking around in amazement. There was no sound and no wind. A few scattered clouds outlined by the starry skies were standing stock-still, "So time across the whole world has stopped? The whole universe?" It was all so impossible, but ne guessed, so was nir shifting.

"I like to think it's more like we have stepped outside the stream of time. As if we are able to stay in a split second for a while. Tess likes to call it *fake time*. I can only keep other people in fake time with me if I touch them, so I stopped time as soon as we heard you were getting into that car and then came and fetched you…."

Indigo nodded, "Ok. Cool. But I still think it is a really good idea if I go with these guys. Finding Arno will be the easiest this way, and they trust me. I should be safe."

"Agreed," Mila didn't even try to argue. "We will go fetch the car and follow behind. Bonnie will be able to track you."

"I'll let Tess know what is happening via the geo-app, but we will leave Abongile out of it for now," Bonnie said. "It would be good to have a bit more information. I'm still not sure what they are planning."

"Whatever it is, I don't like it," Indigo said, "What can they possibly achieve by accusing Arno and his chauffeur of being poachers? It will never stand up in court?"

Bonnie nodded, "It sounds like it is the story they told the guards to keep them compliant. And that Dumisani knows more. There is some plan with the car, but I couldn't quite figure out what."

"And tell Tess about the bunker. I bet you it's near that spot Arno tagged, the reservoir," Indigo suggested.

"Do you think that 'expensive' equipment the guard mentioned might be causing the sound? Would that mean that Dr Kuzmich might be creating that noise intentionally?" Mila asked. "He certainly has a motive…."

Bonnie shook her head, "I would like to think that people are not capable of such horrors. But then, I guess the news says otherwise."

"Let's not speculate too much yet," Indigo said. "First priority is to get Arno safe."

"Roger that," Mila said. "Now go get them, big boy. Zola, was it?"

Indigo laughed, and it sounded abnormally loud in the deathly silence.

"My isiXhosa name," Indigo's smile faded. "Well, I'm very glad you are not going to be too far behind."

Mila nodded, "Nothing will happen to you," was all she said, but sounding so fiercely protective that Indigo felt nemself catching nir breath.

Chapter 33: Tess

Tess checked her iPad for the umpteenth time. Annoyingly, there had been no messages since Indigo and the twins had left to go and find Arno.

Suddenly a message popped up. It was tagged close to the parking lot where Arno had tagged the Mercedes.

> Two guards have picked up the Mercedes. Confirmed that Arno and the chauffeur had been captured, but no eyes on them yet. Following the car now.

"Tess showed the message to Ryan, who gave a low whistle.

"Things are heating up, hey."

As he said it, Nina came stumbling out of the bedroom. She was ash grey and heading straight for the bathroom. Tess could hear her vomiting. Ryan pulled a face, and Tess shook her head in disgust at him. Her gangly friend could happily bring home jars of worms and slugs but was completely freaked out by any bodily fluid.

"What shall we do?" he whispered.

Tess did not answer but listened attentively. It had gone quiet in the bathroom, and she pushed open the door and peeked through. Nina was lying on the floor, breathing much faster than usual, her eyes at half-mast.

"Nina!" she shouted and rushed over.

"I'm ok," Nina whimpered, "I just need to lie here for a little bit."

"No way, my girl," Ryan said. "You are not ok. Enough now, *jirre*. Tess, you call the ambulance, and I'm fetching Alex."

Tess looked at Ryan. No sign of panic. Just clear resolve. She liked this side of him, but it only seemed to arise when the banana had properly hit the fan. Tess was totally freaked out by Nina's condition but put on a brave face as she replied, "Good plan, Ryan. Please bring me my phone and a blanket. I will wait here with Nina."

Ryan nodded and quickly did as he was asked before heading out the door.

Tess sat down on the floor, her back leaning against the bath. Nina put her head on Tess' lap, and Tess tucked the blanket in around her.

"I'm sorry I'm causing all this trouble,"

"Shush now," Tess said. "This is not trouble. There is nothing else we should be doing anyway."

But inside, she was in turmoil. What about Indigo and the twins? She must let them know what is happening. But maybe only in a little bit. They had enough to sort out on their end and needn't be worried about this yet.

As long as Nina was going to be ok.

Madeleine Muller

Chapter 34: *Arno*

Arno swallowed nervously and tried not to cry. He couldn't believe this was happening. Mr Nel had called more guards, and they had tied Lerato and Arno's wrists in front of them with cable ties. The large man had taken their bags and phones but, fortunately, had not opened the devices to check what they had been up to. Arno did not think it would be good if Mr Nel picked up on the geo-tagging app.

Shortly after they had been caught, Mr Nel had called Dr Kuzmich but had walked away to discuss what was to be done. Arno wondered if Dr Kuzmich had still been in the dining room with Jimmy when he got the call. It was getting late. What would Jimmy do? But then Mr Brandt would have been there as well. And surely *he* would not let anything happen to Lerato or him. After all, who would drive home his Mercedes?

Mr Nel had returned after his call looking grim but said no more while marching them through the bush to some unknown destination. Arno had lost all sense of direction but was fairly sure they were heading away from that reservoir he had tagged. At least they had confirmed that something fishy was certainly going on. And most importantly, Jimmy was not with him. As long as Jimmy was ok, nothing else mattered. Arno wondered if Jimmy would tell someone if he did not come home tonight. He knew Jimmy cared, but he was such a coward.

No, of course, he would let someone know.

Arno just hoped he would not leave it too late.

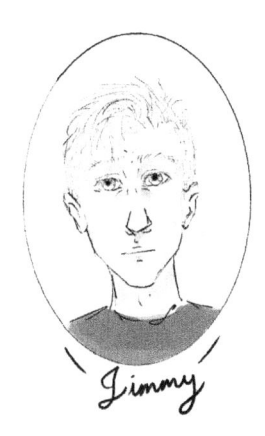

Chapter 35: *Jimmy*

Jimmy stumbled through the dark and headed away from the restaurant and the cluster of cottages. He had to shake off Dr Kuzmich, although he was unsure if the old man was even pursuing him. He looked around, but no one came bursting through the restaurant's front door.

Guess it would look suspicious if he did.

Jimmy kept running till he had cleared the perimeter of the neat gardens and was crashing through untouched veldt.

He stopped and sunk down on his knees in the pitch dark, oblivious of the state of his fancy new suit.

Now what?

He knew he had to get help, but his head was in a whirl, and he could feel a full-blown panic attack coming on.

This was not a good time to freak out.

Tears poured down Jimmy's cheeks.

What if something terrible has happened to Arno?

Jimmy could not imagine his life without his friend. Arno was the only light in his miserable life. The only one who made everything else bearable.

Jimmy took a deep breath and started the five-four-three-two-one.

He had to calm down.

Madeleine Muller

It felt like forever to still his heart a little and to find the strength to stand up. He looked back at the settlement of rondawels, the low lights lighting up the pathways.

He knew what he had to do, but he would have to go back the long way around. Softly, he crept through the veldt, stumbling here and there over dead branches and clumps of grass, but he was too nervous to switch on the flashlight on his phone. Finally, Jimmy reached his destination - the cottage Abongile was sleeping in. With relief Jimmy noticed that the lights were still on inside.

He crouched down behind a small hedge a few metres away and scouted out the environment. Everything seemed quiet, but as he was about to approach the cottage, Dr Kuzmich appeared, rubbing his hands and looking around furtively. Jimmy ducked back down and clamped his hands over his own mouth.

Oh no, oh no, oh no.

Jimmy could hear the knock echoing through the silence and then Abongile's voice. "*Ngubani?*[71]"

"Sorry, Abongile. This is Dr Kuzmich here. Apologies for bothering you so late, but we have a small emergency on our hands."

Jimmy felt relief wash over him. Maybe he got it all wrong, and Dr Kuzmich was not plotting some evil plan. Why else come to Abongile? Arno might get into a spot of trouble, but Abongile would make sure he would be alright.

Unless Abongile worked for Dr Kuzmich.

Jimmy felt cold confusion wash over him.

Had he missed something essential? Was Abongile a bad guy after all? What did he really know about the large ranger?

Jimmy heard the door open.

"Can I come in?" Dr Kuzmich asked.

"Yes, of course, Doctor. Please, do come inside. How can I help?"

The door closed, and Jimmy could hear nothing further. He was too terrified to crawl closer.

Should he go and interrupt them? Challenge Dr Kuzmich?

But if Abongile was in Dr Kuzmich's employ, that would be a disaster.

---

[71] Who is there?

Superheroes in Sterkstroom

Jimmy waited. There did not seem to be anything else to do. It was close to 10.00 p.m. when Abongile and Dr Kuzmich emerged from the rondawel, and Abongile headed straight for his Range Rover.

"Thank you, Abongile. I am sure you will be able to get to the bottom of this," Dr Kuzmich said.

"No problem," Abongile said, getting in and closing the door. Jimmy's heart sank as Abongile's vehicle headed down the drive, Dr Kuzmich watching him go.

Bad guy or good guy, it didn't matter. Abongile was out of the picture.

Jimmy peered through the hedge and watched as Dr Kuzmich looked around carefully before heading off. He felt close to tears. Perhaps it was time to talk to his father… Jimmy shook his head.

That could backfire big time.

A noise startled him, and out of the dark appeared one of those kids, the long-legged coloured boy. He ran un to Abongile's rondawel, banging loudly on the door.

This time Jimmy did not hesitate. He had to trust someone. And even though this was just a kid, anyone was better than his dad. He jumped up and hurtled over the fence.

The kid screamed in fright.

"*Hiert! Wat de hoenner…?*[72]"

And at the same time, the door to the rondawel opened. The blonde-haired vet, a bag slung over her shoulder, stepped out. Jimmy hadn't realised that she would also be there. She held her hand over her heart as she said, "Good grief, what is going on tonight?"

"Sorry. Sorry," Jimmy said. "My name is Jimmy. I need your help."

"Ja, well, get in line, hey," the kid said, putting out his hand as he turned to the vet. "It's Nina, Alex. She's really ill, hey. Tess is calling the ambulance. *Kom asseblief*[73]."

Jimmy felt embarrassment wash over him. Someone was ill and needed help. Why should these people help him? He was just some random stranger. Jimmy felt the chill of isolation.

---

[72] **Hey, what the chicken…**

[73] **Please come.**

Madeleine Muller

The vet looked at Jimmy carefully before she said, "Oh dear! I was just on my way over. Jimmy, why don't you come with us and I will see how I can help. Let me just attend to this girl first."

Jimmy nodded and stayed mute as they headed towards the kids' rondawel. The boy, apparently called Ryan, was explaining to Alex about how this girl Nina was vomiting and drowsy, but Jimmy wasn't listening. The vet did not pay him any further attention, seemingly unperturbed by his presence, and Jimmy wondered if she assumed he was there about a sick animal. Vets were probably used to getting disturbed by strangers at odd times of the night. There was no sign of Dr Kuzmich, which was probably a good thing.

Jimmy thought of Arno, and his heart fluttered. They were running out of time. And would these people be able to do anything? Would he be able to make them understand?

And poor Arno. He must be terrified. Jimmy suddenly wished there were some way he could let Arno know that he was going to make a plan. He was coming for him.

Superheroes in Sterkstroom

Indigo

Chapter 36: *Indigo /Zola*

Indigo sat slouched back in the passenger seat of the Mercedes. Shifting into another shape was more than just a disguise. It was easy to slip into the mannerisms and traits of the body you were wearing. Ne was leaning on nir elbow and hanging out of the rolled-down window while making jokes with Dumisani. Madoda was sulking in the back seat.

Dumisani was driving at a snail's pace. He was either not used to driving or nervous about arriving wherever the hell they were going.

"*So, are you new then?*" Dumisani asked.

"*Yes, this is my first assignment for the company,*" Indigo replied, "*What's this Mr Nel like then? He a good boss?*"

Madoda snorted from the back seat, "*Good? That man? No, that man is what I call a nasty piece of work. The kind of man who used to do the National Party's dirty work. Security forces, I'm telling you.*"

Dumisani shook his head, "*There is no proof of that, Madoda. It's all just rumours. And the man speaks isiXhosa like a local.*"

"*That means nothing, and you know it. It just means he can insult you in your own language. I'm telling you, tonight's business is nasty business,*" Madoda said, getting more and more agitated.

"*Surely we are only turning over a couple of poachers to the Green Scorpions. I hear they are around,*" Indigo said, hoping to poke the bear. At the mention of the Green Scorpions, Dumisani almost drove off the road.

"*Green Scorpions? What are you saying about the Green Scorpions? There are no Scorpions here?*"

"*I don't know,*" Indigo said, "*I saw their Range Rover parked at the Mpangwa Reserve. Don't they deal with poachers?*"

Madoda poked his head between the two seats, "*What did I tell you, Dumisani. I don't want no trouble with the Scorpions. Zola is speaking the truth. Why is Mr Nel not just turning over these guys to the cops? Why make so-called 'special arrangements'.*"

"*Special arrangements?*" Indigo asked, but felt a cold sweat break out on nir forehead. This did not bode well.

"*I don't know,*" Dumisani said, "*But I am getting tired of your paranoia, Madoda. All I know is that we deliver this car to Mr Nel, and then we can skedaddle. The rest is none of our business.*"

Before Indigo could ask for more details, Dumisani slowed down, and Indigo noticed a group of people waiting by the roadside. Lit up by the headlights was a big, white man in civvies, clearly the infamous Mr Nel. Behind him were Arno and Lerato, their hands tied in front of them with cable ties. Arno looked close to tears, but Lerato had a calm, resigned look on his face like he was biding his time. There were three more guards, all in the same security uniforms.

Dumisani parked the Mercedes carefully next to the road, and the three of them got out of the car, Madoda hanging back. Mr Nel looked at Indigo, his eyes narrowing.

This was it. Ne had to convince Mr Nel that ne was legit.

Mr Nel barked, "*En wie de hel is die*[74]?"

But before Indigo could answer, Dumisani replied, "This is Zola, Mr Nel. Dr Kuzmich sent him. He is a new guy, and he says he has no problem helping."

---

[74] And who the hell is this?

Mr Nel looked Indigo up and down. Indigo nervously hopped from foot to foot. Important to look the part, and no doubt, meeting a supervisor as intimidating as Mr Nel would have any guy anxious.

"*Dr Kuzmich sent you, hey?*" Mr Nel asked, in flawless isiXhosa.

Indigo nodded and decided to take a risk. "*I've done some work for him before. On the side....*" Indigo loaded the sentence with innuendo. If ne could convince Mr Nel that ne was happy to do the dirty work….

Mr Nel nodded knowingly.

Great. He had taken the bait.

"*Excellent. Zola, is it? Glad to hear Dr Kuzmich is offering some extra assistance. Dumisani, Madoda, thank you for bringing the car, but you can go back to the bunker now. We will take it from here.*"

Dumisani and Madoda did not need to be asked twice and headed down the track into the bush without as much as a backward glance. Indigo looked at Arno, but the youth was oblivious to the conversations going on around him and had not even considered 'Zola' to be anything more than another guard.

"*What do you want me to do, boss?*" Indigo asked.

"Can you drive?" Mr Nel asked in English. Indigo nodded. "Good. Zola, you and Fandi here will bring the Mercedes. We will put these two in the back seat. The rest of us will take my bakkie. Just follow me."

Only now did Indigo notice the Toyota Hilux double cab up ahead.

Ne could only hope that Bonnie had gotten all of that and that they were not too far behind….

Madeleine Muller

Chapter 37: Tess

Tess heard Alex and Ryan come in and let out a sigh of relief. Nina had fallen asleep. Alex came into the bathroom, picked up Nina and carried her to the couch in the front lounge.

With surprise, Tess noticed a young man standing in the living room, Mr Brandt's son. Tess wondered if he knew about Arno. And whose side was he on, anyway? His dad's or Arno's?

Alex was examining Nina and murmuring soft words of encouragement. Tess looked the young man up and down. He was dressed in a fancy suit, but it was filthy, with grass streaks on the knees - and he was deadly pale, swallowing nervously.

Ryan spoke, "Jimmy arrived when I got to Alex's. Said he needed help *nogal*." He said it casually, all the while giving Tess interesting signals of alarm with his eyes. Tess left Nina with Alex; she was in good hands now and headed to Jimmy.

"Come out to the stoep, Jimmy. You look like you need some fresh air," Tess said in her sweetest voice.

Jimmy looked like he was about to protest, but Tess gave him one of her withering looks, and that shut him up quickly. There was a sliding door that opened on a small protected stoep on the side of the cottage.

Ryan followed them surreptitiously and carefully closed the door behind them.

"Ok. What's going on?" Tess asked.

Jimmy swallowed a couple of times, looking back and forth between Ryan and Tess. He was out of school and a few years older than them, but he looked like a naughty kid in a principal's office. Tess had lost all patience, but Ryan was more sympathetic.

"It's ok, *bra*. Is this about Arno, hey?"

Tess tried to smile encouragingly but was ready to scream in impatience. Jimmy nodded,

"Ja. I think something terrible has happened. And I don't know what to do."

"Tell us what you know. All of it," Tess commanded. It looked like he was an ally, after all.

In fits and starts, Jimmy told them the events of the evening. He told them of how he had stumbled upon a conversation with Dr Kuzmich that hinted at some dodgy business behind the dam; of how Arno had told him about the noise freaking out the animals and had gone to investigate, and then about Dr Kuzmich's mysterious phone call. But the strangest of all was the story of Abongile's conversation with the doctor and his sudden departure.

"No way," Ryan said, "Abongile is fully legit. For sure, hey."

Just then, the sliding door opened, and Alex was glaring at the three of them.

"What are you all up to? And when did that ambulance say it was coming, Tess?"

"Is she ok?" Tess asked in a small voice.

Alex looked over her shoulder at Nina lying on the couch. She seemed to have fallen asleep again.

"Her blood sugar is twenty-six," Alex said, tears welling up.

"What's it s'posed to be?" Ryan asked, and Tess looked at Alex in alarm. Why was Alex crying?

"I've had to double-check the reference range for humans. And Google says it should be under eleven. I think… I think Nina might have diabetes."

Ryan shook his head vehemently, "No way. She does not even like sweets like. And she actually eats green stuff."

Tess watched as Alex tried to pull herself together and put up a brave face. This scared her even more.

Alex explained, "Diabetes in children is usually a genetic thing, Ryan. Nothing to do with diet. But right now, these high sugar levels are poisoning her. She needs to get to a hospital as soon as possible."

And as if for the first time, Alex noticed Jimmy.

"Sorry, Jimmy. I completely forgot about you. What was the problem?"

Tess intervened before Jimmy could say a word.

"He was actually looking for Abongile. It has to do with his friend, Arno...."

"Oh, yes," Alex said, suddenly looking very uncomfortable. "Abongile is actually out looking for your friend. I'm sure everything will be fine."

"Why? What happened?" Tess asked.

Alex shrugged distractedly, clearly still thinking about Nina.

"That man from the Park's Board came round just now. Apparently, Arno and Mr Brandt's chauffeur have taken the car and have gone on some.... let's just say some mission somewhere outside the reserve. Dr Kuzmich asked Abongile to go and investigate."

"What kind of mission?" Tess asked. "And are you sure they have left Mpangwa?"

"I don't know, Tess," Alex said, but it was clear she was hiding something. "But yes. Abongile headed out on the road towards Cathcart to see if he could head them off."

Suddenly, there was a knock on the door, and Tess scooted past Alex to open up. It was the paramedics. They hadn't even heard the ambulance arrive. As soon as the paramedics came in, Alex forgot about everything else and explained to them her limited understanding of what was happening. The paramedic rechecked Nina's sugar, and Tess noticed how quickly they put up a drip.

Jimmy touched Tess' shoulder, and she turned round. He whispered, "Dr Kuzmich is lying. No way Arno would have left the reserve. He was definitely heading for the dam. It must have been a ruse to get Abongile out of the way. I need to go and tell my dad or call the police or something. Do you know anything about what is going on? Where is Arno?"

Tess shook her head and wondered how much she should tell him. She looked back at Nina, who was being loaded onto a stretcher. Nina would need her; she couldn't stay here. There was only so much she could do. Tess grabbed both Ryan and Jimmy by the arm and shuttled them into the corner of the room. Alex and the two paramedics were so busy with Nina that they were not paying them any attention.

"Ok, listen. Jimmy, I'm sorry to say, but Arno and your chauffeur were captured. And definitely on the Mpangwa property. Not sure what happened exactly, but my sisters and their friend have tracked them down and are following them. We don't know how deep Dr Kuzmich and Mr Brandt are involved, but there is something funny going on, especially if Mr Kuzmich is making up stories. I have to go with Nina, so you and Ryan will have to provide backup here."

Jimmy had gotten more and more alarmed as Tess had continued and was stuttering in protest.

"You m..m..mean those twin girls? What the f..f..fudge. That's ridiculous! What the hell are they going to do?"

Just then, Alex called Tess, "Come. We need to go. I will bring the car. Tess, I want you to go in the ambulance with Nina."

"Sure," Tess said and then turning to Ryan, "I will leave my iPad here. You stay glued to the geo-tagging app. And ping them with a message about Dr Kuzmich sending Abongile away."

"Shall I tell them about Nina?" Ryan asked. Tess bit her lip. This was almost too big a decision.

"Maybe. Ja. I don't know."

"I think we have to," Ryan said, putting his hand on Tess' shoulder. Tess nodded and handed over the iPad.

Ryan could handle this.

She ran to the bedroom to get her bag and heard Ryan say to Jimmy, "Now, bra, just relax. And let me tell you a little about these chicks and the awesome dude that is with them.

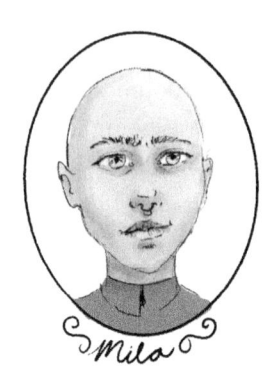

Chapter 38: *Mila*

Mila was driving so slowly that the car was almost stalling, and she had to sit on the clutch to keep the motor running.

"Can't we go a bit faster?" she asked. Bonnie was sitting forward in her seat, her hands on the front of the dashboard.

"Sorry. They are going very slowly. And they've stopped a couple of times. I really don't want them to know we are here. I don't know how you can see anything. It is so dark."

They were driving with the parking lights on, which gave them just enough light to stay on the road. Indigo was somewhere ahead, driving the Mercedes with Arno and the chauffeur in the back. According to what Bonnie could detect from tuning into Indigo's thoughts, the Mercedes was following a double-cab bakkie with the guy in charge and a couple of guards.

The trick with Indigo had worked remarkably well. Bonnie had found tuning into Indigo's head super easy, and she was able to listen to everything Indigo was saying or thinking as if she was sitting in the car right next to her.

"Anything from Tess?" Mila asked, mostly to break the silence.

Bonnie took out her phone to check and let out a shocked gasp. Mila frowned. Bonnie had gone white.

Superheroes in Sterkstroom

"Stop the car," Bonnie said. Without a word, Mila pulled over to the side of the road and switched off the vehicle. Bonnie passed her the phone.

There was a message on the geo-tagging app sent from the rondawel.

> Nina on her way to the hospital with Alex and Tess. Blood sugar very high. Jimmy Brandt here. Told us that Dr Kuzmich sent Abongile off the reserve to go and find Arno and the chauffeur in Cathcart. How are you doing? From Ryan

'Mila's heart contracted at the thought of little Nina being ill. Nina always looked after everyone else. That wasn't fair. She turned to Bonnie, who was crying.

"What do you want to do, sis?"

"We should be with Nina," Bonnie said.

"We should," Mila agreed, "but the doctors are better at managing high sugar, whatever that means, than you or me. And Alex and Nina are with her." Mila hesitated before continuing, "But Bonnie, I don't think Arno and Indigo will manage without us." Mila said this quietly, matter-of-factly. She understood Bonnie knew all of this. Her sister was just processing.

Bonnie has always had a real soft spot for that kid, Mila thought.

Bonnie wiped her eyes with her fingers and sniffed a couple of times. For all their fancy suits and equipment, neither of them had a tissue.

"Sorry. Just got a fright. Of course, you are right." She closed her eyes for a few seconds, "We better get going. They are quite a bit ahead of us now and are speeding up. I think they have left the reserve and are on one of the main roads."

Mila started the car and set off. She tried not to think about what was happening to Nina.

But they had to focus on the present: rescuing Arno and that old man, and keeping Indigo safe.

Madeleine Muller

Chapter 39: *Indigo*

Indigo noticed nir knuckles, white from clenching the steering wheel and tried to will nemself to relax. It was deadly quiet in the car. The other guard in the passenger seat was dosing off. Arno and Lerato had been whispering to each other at first, but the guard had shut them up. Ne wondered what they must be thinking. Arno looked like he had calmed down a little and the old man, Lerato, seemed super-awake and observant.

They had left the reserve and had turned onto the tar road. It was a lonely road, snaking through endless hills, and the Range Rover ahead was doing an easy 120 km an hour. Indigo had panicked that the twins might have lost nem, but not long after the turn, ne had heard Bonnie's voice in nir head.

"*We are right behind you. No worries.*"

Indigo relaxed a little bit. They are going to need backup. The further they drove, the dodgier the whole thing was getting. It occurred to nem that there might be cellphone signal now that they had left the reserve. Indigo tried to think the thought as loudly as ne could, not sure if it would work, "*Try to WhatsApp Abongile - send him a location.*"

Almost immediately, Indigo heard Bonnie's voice, "*Good idea. On it.*"

Indigo smiled.

This was better than cellphones.

Madeleine Muller

Chapter 40: *Arno*

Arno was trying to remember how to do the five-four-three-two-one. He always talked Jimmy through it, but he was struggling to remember the order. You started with things you could see and then things you could hear, but after that, it was a bit hazy. But he was already beginning to calm a little.

One can only panic for so long, hey.

He had felt a small flutter of anxiety when they left the reserve, but maybe it was better they were on a public road. Surely out here, they were more likely to get help? The grumpy guard in the passenger seat had fallen asleep, and the new guy that was driving had a faint smile on his face. He didn't seem too scary.

"Excuse me, Mister," Arno said and cleared his throat, "But do you know where we are going, hey?" The sleeping guard stirred but did not wake.

Zola didn't look around but replied happily enough, "Just following orders, boy. But no need to worry. The police will sort this all out."

"The police?" Arno was sceptical. It would be great if they were on their way to the police, but surely the police would have come to pick them up at the reserve.

Superheroes in Sterkstroom

And then the guard said something unexpected, "We only operate in the confines of the law, boy." He sped up slightly to stay in sight of Mr Nel's Hilux.

"Really?" Arno said, "Corse this don't feel very legal to me. And that man, Mr Nel, took my phone. I want my phone call."

Perhaps this guard could be of some help....

"I will make sure you get it," the man replied, and Arno felt a small stirring of hope. He didn't seem too bad. If they had at least one person who would protest on their behalf if things went south... Arno sat back and made eye contact with Lerato. The old man's eyes flicked downwards, and Arno followed his gaze. Lerato was quietly rubbing his hands together, tied together as if in prayer, and slowly the cable tie was forwarding bit by bit over his hands. Lerato gave him a pointed look. Arno nodded slightly and moved as close as possible to the window, keeping his hands low. The cable tie pinched painfully, but Arno could feel it moving as he copied Lerato's moves. Where did the old man learn to do that? He nervously looked at the guards, but they seemed oblivious to what was happening in the back seat, the one dude still sleeping.

A couple of minutes later and Lerato's hands were loose. He dropped the cable tie on the floor and kept his hands pressed together. With the long sleeves of his overall, it was not obvious that he was untied unless you looked closely. Arno kept patiently at it, but the cable tie was painfully wedged halfway down his hands.

Suddenly, with no warning, the Hilux pulled off the road, and the driver manoeuvred the Mercedes behind it. The moon had come out, and Arno could see some sort of bridge ahead. There was a sign that Arno couldn't make out.

"It's the *Henny Stein Bridge*," Lerato said, "This is the *Orange River*."

"You shut up!" the guard who had been sleeping said, woken up by the car stopping. Arno's misgivings increased.

"I'll go see what's going on," the driver said and got out. The other guard was awake and looking around, and Arno did not dare move any further, the cable tie digging painfully into the back of his hands. He closed his eyes and thought of Jimmy.

Madeleine Muller

When he had been in Grade 11, there had been a time when Arno had been hopelessly in love with Jimmy. But he had never let on. At first, it was a nightmare, trying to negotiate friendship and staying cool, but Arno discovered that by journaling, he could slowly reason himself out of the folly of falling for a straight boy. Only madness lay that way. By matric, he had found himself a gorgeous cricket player, first team *nogal*. Nothing too serious but enough to nip that little obsession in the bud.

But now Arno wondered. How could you just stop loving someone? Perhaps all he had done was manage his own expectations, and that had made their friendship possible.

Arno was no longer hoping for a rescue. Nothing good could come from stopping at one of the biggest rivers in South Africa. He was going to die and would never have told Jimmy that Jimmy had been his everything, his person, his salvation… from that first day they met.

Arno sighed.

Did it really matter? Would it not just have complicated things?

He was surprised at how calm he felt, as if the whole thing was just a strange, surreal dream and he, an innocent bystander watching it all unfold.

He really should be panicking.

Arno tried to imagine his funeral and hoped his friends would do right by him with rainbow flags and lots of Abba. A proper kitch pride parade. Not even these images rattled him, but then he looked at Lerato, and it was the thought of Lerato's funeral that did the trick.

Cold fear washed over Arno, and for a moment, Arno felt completely paralysed, like a deer in headlights.

But he was no blerrie deer. And he was not going to go quietly.

The guard had closed his eyes and was dozing again. Slowly Arno started rubbing his hands together.

This was not over till the fat lady sang.

And it was Gloria Gaynor, singing '*I'll survive*'….

Chapter 41: *Nina*

Nina was lying in a bed at the emergency unit of the Sterkstroom Provincial Hospital. It was a government hospital, the private hospital in Queenstown just too far away for comfort. The cubicle she was in wasn't fancy, with some peeling paint on the green walls and the stained curtains pulled closed around the bed with several hooks missing, but it was clean, and a lovely large night nurse called Patience was fussing over her.

Nina looked at the needle inserted into the back of her hand with a strange feeling of disconnection. As if it wasn't her hand that was connected to a pipe and a bag of fluid slowly dripping salt water into her veins. She was so tired and feeling super sleepy and wide awake all at the same time. Tess appeared and gave her a small, concerned smile. She had been waiting in the passage whilst Patience had put up the drip.

"Hey. How are you feeling?"

Nina tried to give Tess a reassuring smile, but it felt exhausting to pretend, "A little bit better. I'm not so nauseous now. And it is so quiet." It was only as she said it that she realised the truth of it.

"What do you mean?" Tess asked.

"That noise. I can't hear it here. I mean, I didn't actually hear it when we were at Mpangwa, but I think it was there all the time. Like a hum in the background that I couldn't get away from. But now…" Nina sighed,

"Now it's better. But you need to tell me what's going on, Tess? That boy was there when the ambulance fetched me."

"Oh, yeah." Tess said, "That is Jimmy. He was worried about Arno."

Nina tried to sit upright, "What happened to Arno? What's going on, Tess?"

"Wow. Relax, Nina. It's fine." Nina's suspicions grew as Tess continued, "Arno did get into a spot of trouble, but Indigo and the twins are sorting it out. Indigo is with him now."

Nina studied Tess carefully. She knew Tess was not telling her the full story but did it really matter? If Mila and Bonnie were there, it would all be fine.

"Anyway, Ryan and Jimmy are on it for any backup if needed." This made Nina smile, "I'm sure Ryan is in his element."

Tess laughed, "Ja, hey. We are never going to hear the end of it. But Ryan was really cool when you got sick. They'll be fine."

Nina put out her right hand, the one without all the contraptions connected to it, and Tess took it. Nina said,

"Tess. And what is going on with me, exactly? I didn't quite follow some of the stuff the doctor was saying. She took blood to go and test and said she would explain more later, but what does this all mean? I heard Alex say my sugar was too high."

"I think we must just wait for the doctor," Tess said, looking nervously at the closed curtains.

Nina scoffed, "Oh, come on, Tess. I am sure you've been eavesdropping on Alex and the doctor's conversations - and probably Googled it. Please tell me. I know it's not… not good…."

Tess sighed and sat down on the side of the bed,

"Nina, even the doctor doesn't have all the answers yet. The blood tests will tell more. But Alex was fairly sure that with your sugar being so high, you might have diabetes."

Tess pressed her lips together as if stifling a sob. Nina tried to wrack her brain. She didn't know anything about diabetes, except that you couldn't eat sweets.

"But isn't it usually old people that have diabetes? Like your granny had?"

Tess shook her head, "There are different types. Kids get something called type 1 diabetes. It's like a genetic thing. And it causes your pancreas to stop making this hormone called insulin. Granny Jenny says that your mom's cousin had the same thing."

Nina's eyes widened, "You spoke to Granny Jenny?"

"Oh, no. Alex did. Geez, Nina, we obviously had to call your grandmother. Maria will bring her through tomorrow… But don't worry, ok. They have medicines to treat diabetes these days. You are going to be fine…."

Tess went quiet and shifted uncomfortably on the bed.

"Ok, Tess. What are you not telling me?" Nina asked. She knew her friend too well. Tess sighed and squeezed her hand a bit harder.

"The medicine to treat the diabetes… you are going to have to have insulin every day to keep your sugar under control. And the problem is… it only comes in injections."

Nina frowned, "I don't like needles, Tess. Don't say I am going to have to have an injection every day?"

Tess winced, "Well, the thing is. You may have to inject a few times a day, every day."

Nina welled up with tears and shook her head. It seemed so completely impossible that this could be happening to her. Only a few days ago, she had felt fine. Maybe she had become a bit thinner over the last two months, but Maria had said it was because of her growth spurt. How could she have some horrible serious illness? It didn't seem real.

Tears spilt over Nina's cheeks, and Tess threw her arms around her friend's neck, sobbing loudly, "I'm so sorry, Nina. I'm so sorry."

Nina gently pushed Tess back so that she could wipe her eyes with the back of her hand - it was tricky only having one hand available to do stuff with, "It's not your fault, Tess."

"But what if it is?" Tess said, clearly in distress, "What if it is this sound that made you ill?"

Nina shook her head, "You just said it was a genetic thing. And I've been thinking. I've not been a hundred per cent for a couple of months now. Even Ryan said I was getting too thin. The sound might have made things worse, but I don't think it caused it, Tess."

Tess nodded, and Nina wondered how much Tess had been blaming herself since this had all happened.

But talking about the sound suddenly brought back the image of the little shrub hare and all those animals suspended in time.

"Tess," Nina said, grabbing her friend's arm, "you have to make sure we figure out what is going on. We have to help those animals."

Tess smiled through her tears, "Don't worry. I haven't even told you yet, but we think we know what is causing that noise. It is all being sorted out."

Just then, Patience returned, her large brown face filled with warmth and concern, "*Haibo mntwana*[75]. You mustn't upset your friend now. She needs to rest."

And then to Nina, "Hello, my little one. I need to check your sugar now and give you an injection. The doctor will be here soon to come and check on you."

Tess got up to leave, and Nina gave her a smile.

"Don't worry about me, Tess. I've got you and Ryan, and granny and Maria are coming tomorrow. And at home, Toast, Aero and Captain Henry are waiting. With all of you caring for me, I know I'm going to be ok."

Tess went over and kissed her on the forehead before saying to Patience, "Mama, please be gentle with my friend."

Patience was preparing the lancet to prick Nina's finger but looked up briefly, "*Sukuzikhataza*[76], Tess. I have a special trick when I test for blood sugar. Nina won't feel a thing.

---

[75] **No way, child**
[76] **Dont worry yourself**

Superheroes in Sterkstroom

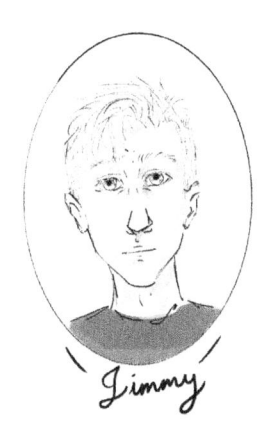

Chapter 42: *Jimmy*

Jimmy and Ryan sat on the couch in the rondawel, staring at the geo-tagging app. Bonnie had replied to their message, and Jimmy kept re-reading it.

> Send our love to Nina. Keep us posted. We are following Arno. Leaving Mpangwa now via East gate

"Are you sure these people know what they are doing?" Jimmy asked. He had asked different versions of this same question at least three other times. But it was all so far-fetched. Superheroes? No way.

But it was uncanny how these three teens were able to track the men who had taken his friend.

Ryan sighed, "I'm telling you, bra, Mila and Bonnie are full-on legit. I've seen them in action. And Indigo. I don't even know all the stuff that dude can do."

"I'm… I'm just really worried," Jimmy said in a small voice. "I feel so useless just sitting here whilst Arno is in danger."

"I know, bra. You love him, hey," Ryan said matter-of-factly.

Jimmy hesitated, "Yes, well, no. Not like that. Or maybe just a little bit like that." Jimmy felt his face heat up. He had never admitted before that his friendship with Arno was anything more than just platonic, not even to himself.

Ryan put his hand on Jimmy's shoulder, "Arno's gonna be fine. Pinky promise, my bra. We just gotta sit tight."

Just then, the app tinged. The location was on one of the main roads, not far from the Orange River.

'Can't reach Abongile. Our messages not being delivered. Reception terrible. Two vehicles with four men have stopped at the Hennie Stein bridge. Armed! Lerato and Arno fine. Please try to reach Abongile / Police."

Ryan whipped out his phone and sent a message to Abongile via WhatsApp, but it stayed on a single tick - undelivered. He tried calling, but every call was dropped. Jimmy noticed Ryan getting more and more alarmed. The boy looked at Jimmy with large eyes and said in a low whisper.

"I don't know what to do. If the girls are calling for backup, things are bad."

"I have an idea," Jimmy said, "Mr Dumani was bragging about their two-way radio system. He uses it to stay in touch with all the game drive guides. Each vehicle has one. I'm sure the Green Scorpions have radios as well."

" Ja, hey. I saw one of those cool radios in Abongile's car. Do you think we can ask Mr Dumani to use his? It's very late," Ryan's eyes were shining.

Jimmy was already on his feet, "Come. We will wake Mrs Braithwaite. We can tell her that something has happened to Arno. She will definitely help. And if we can't reach Abongile, we'll call the police.

Ryan closed the iPad and stood up, "Now we are talking. Sittin' here on our arses is driving me bananas."

The two youths grabbed some warm clothes, and Ryan quickly packed a bag with flashlights and a few basics. As they headed out the door, Ryan stopped Jimmy.

Superheroes in Sterkstroom

"We are gonna get Arno back, no worries, bra. And I don't know much about love and such, like, but I think you need to tell Arno how you feel, dude. You two make a really awesome couple." And with that, Ryan headed off towards Mrs Braithwaite's cottage.

Jimmy followed, shaking his head.

The word 'couple' had sent a tingle down his spine. But that was just plain crazy. He wasn't gay. There was even that girl he had a crush on in Grade 11. Jimmy tried to remember her name, but it was all a bit hazy. But then he thought of Arno.

And there was nothing hazy thinking about Arno at all.

Madeleine Muller

Chapter 43: *Indigo*

Indigo walked over to the Hilux but stopped a couple of metres away, looking indecisive. Mr Nel and the two guards had gotten out of the car, and Mr Nel was rifling through a large kit bag in the boot of the vehicle. Indigo kept nir distance, looking uninterested whilst trying to figure out what Mr Nel was planning.

"Everything ok back there, Zola?" Mr Nel asked over his shoulder, now speaking in English.

"*Ja, baas*[77]," Indigo said, not mentioning that Lerato had managed to get out of his ties and that Arno was in the process of undoing his. Indigo carefully counted all visible weapons. Each of the guards had a standard issue revolver on the hip, old fashioned but no less effective. Mr Nel was not visibly armed, but he was wearing a large khaki fleece, and Indigo wouldn't have been surprised if he had a hidden shoulder holster underneath.

"Here we go," Mr Nel said and brought out a large brown bottle and some loose pieces of material. He gestured for Indigo to come closer.

"Now, Zola, you say you are cool, né?"

---

[77] Yes, boss

Superheroes in Sterkstroom

"Ja, baas," Indigo said, making just enough eye contact to look trustworthy but not overconfident. "I've worked for Dr Kuzmich a long time now. We understand each other."

Mr Nel nodded with satisfaction.

"These two people in that car. They are causing trouble, my boy, and they are going to cost Mr Kuzmich a lot of money."

Indigo nodded in rapt attention.

"They are the kind of people nobody will miss. That old black man has no family, no people. And the kid is a *poefter*[78]."

Indigo pulled a face as if to agree with Mr Nel's sentiments on queers. Mr Nel looked over Indigo's shoulder to where Arno and Lerato were sitting, still in the back of the Merc, and then dropped his voice.

"There is going to be a little accident tonight. *Uyaqonda*[79]? Over the edge of this bridge. The river is nice and deep at the moment. We will put the chauffeur behind the wheel and the kid in the front. But we don't want them to make too much fuss, you know, going over."

Mr Nel held up the bottle, and Indigo could just make out the large faded letters on the brown label: *Chloroform*. Ne gave an evil grin.

"Sure, boss. Nice stuff. You sure the police won't find it later?"

Mr Nel scoffed and touched the side of his nose, "Don't worry about that. I know the police inspector in Sterkstroom. They are overworked and understaffed. No one will look too closely."

Indigo nodded and took the chloroform, "Sha'p, my baas. Let me drive the car to the middle of the bridge. *Masihambe*[80]...."

Mr Nel laughed out loud. "That's my boy."

Indigo turned around, feeling slightly sick. How can people do things like this? And ne wondered if Mr Nel had ever murdered anyone in cold blood before. Indigo let the horror of it wash all over nem and then let it go.

Ne was not afraid. Ne had a job to do.

And ne had help.

---

[78] faggot
[79] Do you understand?
[80] Let us go.

Madeleine Muller

Arno

Chapter 44: Arno

Arno tried to figure out what Mr Nel was doing at the back of the Hilux, but the guard called Zola was standing in the way. The large man was getting something out of the boot, but Arno couldn't see what it was. He glanced over to Lerato, who gave him a pointed look. Arno's hands were burning where the cable ties were cutting into his skin, but he continued rubbing his hands together in small movements.
And then suddenly, the cable tie slipped over his knuckles, and Arno dropped it quietly to the ground. He followed Lerato's lead, keeping his hands together as if he was still tied up, and felt a little bit more in control of what was happening.

Mr Nel and the driver finished their conversation, and the driver turned round to head back to the car. He was carrying something in his hand, a bottle of some kind and had a grim look on his face. Arno's heart sank. This was not good.

Arno blinked, and suddenly, there on the seat in front of him was Mila. She was leaning over the back of the driver seat, and she had her hand on his shoulder.

"Howzit, bro," She said.

Arno screamed.

His eyes flicked to the guard, but he was still fast asleep. He whipped his head around to look at Lerato, but things were getting really weird.

Superheroes in Sterkstroom

Lerato was looking straight ahead, his eyes stark, not moving a muscle, not even breathing.

"*Jirre, man. Wat gaan aan?*[81]"

"Breathe," Mila said. "In and out. Everything is fine."

"Am I dead?" Arno asked. "Did I get shot or somethin'? This is not right, hey. Not right at all."

"You are fine," Mila said.

"Oh, for goodness sake, Mila," a voice said, and Arno looked out the car window. Bonnie was there, and next to her that guard Zola. Arno wanted to say something. Warn them or something….

"Arno. Just breathe. Time has been stopped. You are sitting in a moment of frozen time," Bonnie said.

Bonnie tried to open the door, but she was struggling, "Mila, please open this bloody door."

Arno wasn't sure what Mila actually did, but the door swung open, and there was Bonnie, kneeling next to him.

"Everything is suspended, Arno. Look around. A little talent that Mila has."

Arno did as he was told. The guard was not sleeping but actually completely still - just like Lerato. Mila had climbed back out of the Mercedes, and Arno could see Mr Nel frozen in the action of closing the boot, as were the two guards next to him.

And it was quiet, deadly quiet. Arno could hear his own breathing.

"Ok," he said, "Maybe not dead, hey. But dreamin' for sure."

"Come," Bonnie said and helped Arno out of the car.

Softly she rubbed his hands, easing the ache from the cable ties. Arno started crying. He did not know what was happening, but for now, he felt safe, surrounded by these strange young people. It didn't feel like a dream. And he would very much like it not to be.

The guard handed him a handkerchief and gave him a smile. He looked faintly familiar. Arno dried his eyes and looked at Bonnie. They were all patiently waiting for him to calm down. He took a deep breath,

---

[81] Geez man, what's going on?

"*Nou*, I don't know what *de hel* is goin' on here. But I am sure glad to see you. Now you are just gonna have to run over all that again, hey."

Mila laughed, "I told you he'd be fine. Arno is from the Flats - they are tough cookies."

Between Mila and Bonnie, they gave a rather odd explanation of what was happening. He could follow that Mila stopped time, and Bonnie's telepathy seemed perfectly natural, especially in the light of Nina's powers, but when they told him that Indigo had some weird shape-shifting power, it all became a bit too much.

"Ok then. But where are they?"

Zola put his hand up, "Hey, dude. I'm here. I hope you don't mind me shifting back for your gratification. Bit of a hassle, and I might still need the shape for now."

Arno looked at the black man carefully. He had the height of Abongile, but he was thinner, but something of Indigo remained around the eyes.

Arno gave a quick shake of his head, like a dog shaking off water. But they were all still there. Watching him kindly. Waiting.

"So now what?" Arno asked. It felt strange in this 'fake time.' The twins were completely relaxed. There was no rush, no need to do anything.

Indigo stepped forward and showed him the bottle in their hand. "Mr Nel is planning to chloroform you and Lerato and then push the car off this bridge. He has some contacts in the police force that will sign this off as a freak car accident."

"Into the river?" Arno asked, the question obvious, but in his mind, he had an image of him and Lerato in the front seats, sinking into the deep water.

Mila took over, "We need to decide how we are going to play this. We have two options. One, we can simply load you and Lerato into our car and get you all out of here, and leave Mr Nel and his team befuddled and confused when I unfreeze time again...."

Arno nodded. That sounded great.

"...but it will be tricky to explain what happened later, and we probably won't be able to prove what Mr Nel was planning. Or, we pretend to go along with this charade for a bit and let Abongile catch Mr Nel in the act...."

Arno raised his eyebrows, "Wait a sec. Exactly how far in the act would we have to be. I have no interest in a midnight swim, thank you very much."

Mila laughed, "Don't worry, Arno. Remember, we control the narrative. And Abongile is on his way...."

"Jimmy and Ryan have gotten hold of him on a two-radio, can you believe it," Bonnie added.

"Jimmy?" Arno asked, "What do you mean, Jimmy?"

"He has been helping," Bonnie said. "He told us that Dr Kuzmich is involved. Jimmy has been very worried about you. And he has teamed up with Ryan, and they have helped us track down Abongile."

Arno smiled.

Jimmy came through for him. Why had he ever doubted his friend?

"Ok," Arno agreed, "We can't let these bastards get away with blerrie murder, hey? You just make sure that car doesn't go over that edge. For then, Mr Brandt will kill me for sure.

Now, what is the second plan?"

Madeleine Muller

Chapter 45: *Indigo*

Indigo started the car and slowly pulled onto the bridge. Ne made eye contact with Arno in the rearview mirror and nodded. Ne would drive slowly, but they didn't have much time. It had been a bit disorientating when Mila had released time, and ne had to get back into character. Indigo had chased the other guard out of the car, saying ne had 'orders' and it was just the three of them left in the Mercedes. Lerato was quiet, looking unblinking out into the night.

Arno spoke, "*Mamela Tata*[82]."

Indigo watched Lerato's eyes widen in shock, his gaze flicking towards 'Zola'.

"It's fine, Lerato." Arno continued, "In… I mean, Zola is a friend. He is part of the rescue team. Undercover like. He is going to help us. And Abongile is on his way. The cops know where we are."

"*Hayi, bhuti. Andiqondi.*[83]"

Indigo interrupted, "We don't have much time. Mr Nel's plan is to put both of us in the front seat, then put you to sleep by putting a cloth over

---

[82] Listen father

[83] No boy, I don't understand.

your mouth and nose with some medicine on it. And then they are going to push this car over the edge if the bridge…."

"Heibo!" Lerato said. "I will fight…."

"Shush, Lerato," Arno said urgently. "Just listen. We don't have time."

Indigo continued, "I need you to pretend, *Mnumzan*[84]. I need you to follow my orders, get into the car and pretend to fall asleep when I use the cloths. I promise you will be rescued before anything bad can happen."

"But why all this pretence?" Lerato protested. "If you are our friend, why can't we just keep driving and get away from Mr Nel?"

It was a good question and one of the options that had been hotly discussed whilst they had all been in fake time. The problem was that Zola would have to vanish when all this was done and wouldn't be able to serve as a witness to Mr Nel's plans. The whole thing would be really hard to explain. They had to wait till Abongile got here.

"We have to catch these guys, Lerato," Arno said. "They cannot be allowed to get away with this. If we just drive away, we might never be able to prove there was anything dodgy going on."

Lerato shook his head in disgust.

"*Hayi, andiyazi*[85], Arno. This is a crazy, stupid plan. And I don't want to die tonight."

"Everything will be fine," Indigo said, knowing how unconvincing it must sound, "and I will leave the keys in the ignition. If, at any time, things are not going according to plan, you just get Arno out of here. OK?" Lerato sighed and gave a small nod.

They had reached the middle of the bridge, and Indigo switched off the car. Ne scouted out the surroundings.

"I'm so sorry, Lerato," Arno said, "I didn't mean to get us in this much trouble. It was stupid going off without telling anyone."

"You think Mr Brandt knows about this, Arno?" Lerato asked, his voice full of sadness.

---

[84] sir

[85] No, I don't know.

Madeleine Muller

"He is a crook, Lerato, but I don't think he is a monster. I'm sure he wouldn't have allowed anything to happen to either of us. It's Dr Kuzmich behind all this."

Indigo had been watching them talk in the rearview mirror and, with surprise, ne noticed Lerato smiling.

"And Mr Brandt certainly wouldn't let anything happen to his Mercedes."

Arno gave a small laugh, "Hayi, Lerato. That's evil, bra."

Indigo felt the tension in the car give a bit. This was good.

"Ok. Here is the plan…."

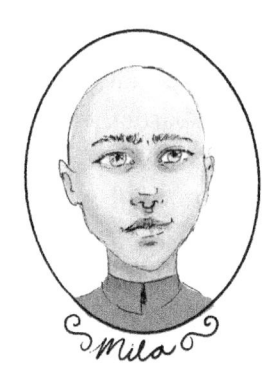

Chapter 46: *Mila*

Mila and Bonnie were hidden behind a clump of bushes right next to where the Hilux was parked. It would not have been much of a hiding place in the day, but in the pitch dark, they were pretty much invisible. Mila had a small set of night binoculars and was following the progress of the Mercedes over the bridge. As soon as Indigo had set off with the two captives, Mr Nel had ordered one of the guards to go down the road and stop any car that might be approaching.

"Tell them there was an accident and to stay in their cars. It will be true soon enough," Mr Nel said before letting out a gruff laugh.

A proper bloody villain, Mila thought.

Mr Nel and the remaining two guards climbed into the Range Rover and headed over the bridge.

"What's their plan, Bonnie?" Mila asked.

"Mr Nel is going to place a guard at the other end of the bridge to stop traffic from that side. This bridge connects the Eastern Cape with the Free State. It's quite a busy main road. Even at this time of night, the odd truck might head this way."

The bridge was incredibly long, over 1.1 km, and even with the binoculars, she could hardly see Mr Nel reach the other side to drop off the other guard before heading back to the middle of the bridge. *So, Mr Nel was willing to get his hands dirty.*

Fortunately, getting the car off the bridge was not going to be a simple matter. The bridge wall was easy enough - it was a metal grid fence that could be dismantled - but on the left side between the fence and the road was a 20 cm high raised concrete barrier, protecting the water pipes that ran alongside the road. It was supposed to be covered by paving, but large sections were missing. A railroad between the road and the bridge edge ran on the right-hand side, so they couldn't push the car off that side. It was going to take time to set it all up.

Mila hoped it would at least be enough time for help to arrive.

She was nervous…the timing was everything, and the biggest risk was the guns. They needed to set it up, so Abongile arrived just before the 'deed was done,' but Mila was worried that Mr Nel and his guards would retaliate if they were suddenly apprehended. A shoot-out would be a disaster.

And Indigo was right in the middle of it all.

Whilst Mr Nel was dropping off the second guard, Mila watched as Indigo stepped out of the car. They had their gun in their hand and were shouting orders to Lerato and Arno. The two got out of the backseat, their hands still held out in front of them as if tied up, and Indigo shoved Lerato into the driver's seat, with Arno into the front passenger seat. Through the binoculars, Mila could see that the two were not nearly as terrified as they should have been under the circumstances, but from a distance, it looked convincing enough. Indigo walked round to the back of the car and used the boot as a table, placing the chloroform on the top and angling it in such a way that Mr Nel would not notice that they hadn't even removed the cap of the bottle whilst 'wetting' the cloths.

Quickly Indigo yanked open the car door and leaned in, first 'drugging' Lerato, who seemingly slumped in his seat, and then Arno. Arno let out a couple of impressive high-pitched screams but then similarly collapsed backwards.

Indigo sauntered over to the bridge edge, kicked the concrete rim a couple of times and then walked over to test the strength of the metal-grid fence as Mr Nel arrived. Mila held her breath as Mr Nel walked over to Indigo. If he checked on Lerato and Arno, it would not take much to realise that they weren't actually unconscious. But Mr Nel seemed more concerned about figuring out how they would stage the accident. Indigo had done well. They had won Mr Nel's trust.

"Mila," Bonnie whispered next to her, and Mila almost jumped out of her skin. Bonnie pointed to the geo-tagging app on her phone. She had been sending messages via the app, with Ryan and Jimmy relaying them to Abongile via the two-way radio, "Abongile is about ten minutes away. And I'm worried about what's going to happen when he arrives. We need to be closer."

Mila nodded.

"Stop," she said, hardly above a whisper.

The first thing you notice when time stops is the quiet. All the sounds you didn't even know were there are suddenly absent. The chirping cicadas, the rustle of small animals in the grass, the slight movement of wind through the leaves.

Dead quiet.

The twins headed over the bridge and into the darkness. A full moon was out, and the road was washed in silvery light, but the bridge was so long that the car was only a distant speck in the dark.

"You are worried," Bonnie said, matter of factly.

"I don't like guns," Mila replied. With Bonnie, you don't need to say much.

"Indigo will be fine," Bonnie said, "It's not all up to you. We are a team, remember. And Indigo is part of that team."

Mila gave her sister a grateful smile. She knew she should be worried about Arno and that poor chauffeur, but only Indigo was in her thoughts.

Mr Nel and the guard were bent over the fence in a perfect tableau. It looked like they were trying to unscrew a section of the metal guard rail. Indigo was leaning against the bonnet of the Mercedes, looking at the men with quiet nonchalance. Their eyes were clear and bright in the moonlight, the only part recognisable as Indigo, and Mila's heart gave a little lurch.

She put her hand on Indigo's shoulder and whispered, "Flow,"

Indigo's eyes flew to hers in shock before they quickly looked around to check, and then they smiled.

"Hey, super chick. What's up?"

Mila smiled back, "Just seeing how you are doing. Everything ok?"

Indigo nodded, "Yip, Arno and Lerato gave a passable performance at passing out, and so far, no one has thought to check up on them. Mr Nel and his pal are going to open up a section of the fence there, and the plan is to lift the damn car over this broken concrete pavement to get it off the bridge. With only three of us, it's going to be a bloody mission. Mr Nel must have a lot of faith in this police inspector because no forensics will confirm that this was an accident."

"I think this whole plan was devised at the spur of the moment. And it means the guys are cagey and unpredictable," Bonnie said.

"How far is Abongile?" Indigo asked.

"About ten minutes. So there should be enough time. That metal fence will not give away easily. But we are worried about what will happen when he arrives." Mila's eyes flicked down to Indigo's gun, now back in its holster. "Do you think we could disable these guns or something?"

Indigo nodded slowly, "Like taking out the bullets, perhaps...?" It was said with just a hint of irony, and Mila blushed, "Yeah. Sorry. Of course. Just take the bullets out," and as an embarrassing afterthought, "I know nothing about guns."

Indigo pulled out their weapon and, with an easy, fluid motion, emptied the chamber.

"Cool. How do you know how to do that?" Mila asked.

"I don't," Indigo said, "but *this body* does."

"How about the guns of the other guys? Would they work all the same?" Bonnie asked.

"Doesn't matter," said Indigo, "I can shift into the hands of each of the guys, including Mr Nel. I should be able to get all the bullets and not leave any dodgy fingerprints in the process."

Mila looked at Indigo in admiration, "That's awesome."

Bonnie laughed, "You sound like Ryan, Mila. Now let's get all these guns emptied, shall we."

Superheroes in Sterkstroom

The three took their time to ensure there were no hidden weapons, but each man had only one gun, and Mr Nel's was in a shoulder holster, as Indigo had suspected. Indigo handed the bullets to Mila, who chucked them over the side of the bridge.

When they were done, Mila turned to Indigo, "Bonnie and I are going to head back to disable that guard's gun and meet Abongile."

"Shouldn't he be arriving about now?" Indigo asked.

"You forgot we stopped time, Indigo. He is still ten minutes away. Once we are back over the bridge, the clock will start again. You ok?" Mila asked, feeling strangely protective.

"Hundreds," Indigo said, "especially since all the bullets are in the Orange River now. Nothing like a stray bullet to ruin a perfectly good rescue."

Bonnie started to head back, but Mila hung back a moment. She and Indigo stood on the bridge, looking out over the gigantic Orange River, bathed in moonlight.

"What a pretty sight," Indigo said. "Wouldn't mind paddling this river someday."

Mila nodded, "Imagine doing the whole of the Orange River, from start to finish. It crosses pretty much most of South Africa. One could just camp on the banks."

"Ja. Great idea. You just need the right team. It would be quite an intense trip - rapids, crocodiles, foreign countries…."

Mila took a deep breath.

Well, here goes nothing,

"I sure wouldn't mind having you on my team, Indigo."

At first, Indigo didn't answer; they just started to make their way back to the Mercedes to take the same position they had been in when Mila had stopped time.

As they leaned back on the bonnet, crossing their arms, they said, "Sure, I would very much like that."

Madeleine Muller

Bonnie

Chapter 47: *Bonnie*

Bonnie helped Mila carry the immobilised guard to the side of the road. The guard was asleep, just like the animals, temporarily suspended in a time bubble. It was certainly the most humane way to get him out of the way. Abongile's phone had finally got some cellphone reception, and Bonnie's phone vibrated in her pocket

> Abongile
> About 5 minutes out from Hennie Steyn

> Bonnie
> Dim your lights and come quietly. We will meet you on the road

Within a couple of minutes, they could hear the car approaching, and Abongile pulled up next to them. He jumped out of the car, and Bonnie could feel the surge of his emotions. He was high on adrenalin and testosterone, a mixture of anger, anxiety and confusion.

Oh, dear.

Superheroes in Sterkstroom

"What the hell is going on here!" Abongile whispered loudly. "Ryan is spouting nonsense about you guys on a rescue mission. I mean, for goodness sake, look at you. All dressed up like some comic book heroes. And what is this Arno kid up to? Dr Kuzmich had a whole story about some exotic animal racket Arno and Lerato are running on the side."

Bonnie could feel Mila tense up. She had no patience with people's emotional overload. She took a deep breath and smiled sweetly.

"Abongile, we are very happy to see you. We have tried to get hold of you, but the reception has been a bitch. Now we can cover all these details later, but what you need to know right now is that Arno went exploring on his own tonight, and he found something, something he was not supposed to. He got caught by Mr Nel from a security company who is taking orders from Dr Kuzmich." Bonnie paused to let that all sink in. Abongile's brow furrowed in confusion, "Ok. So where is Arno now?"

"Arno and Lerato, Mr Brandt's chauffeur, are in the Mercedes in the middle of the bridge. As we understand it, the plan is to drug them using chloroform and to push the car over the edge of the bridge where the river is deepest."

Bonnie could feel Abongile's energy shift. He was no longer confused and had no more questions. Something in him had gone quiet, like a hunter with his prey in sight. Someone was in danger and needed help.

"How do you know all this?"

"We have been following them," Bonnie explained, "And we know one of Mr Nel's guards. He doesn't like what is happening and has been helping us out."

Bonnie could feel Abongile's suspicion, but he asked no further questions. Mila handed him her binoculars and led him around the bend in the road. Best he see for himself.

Mr Nel and the guard had just managed to dismantle one of the metal fence sections, and Mila could see it glistening as they threw it over the edge and into the river. She shivered.

"Shit," Abongile said and then looked at her apologetically. Mila pretended she didn't hear. He continued smoothly, "We will need backup. I'm calling the cops at Ventersdorp. It's not too far from here and I know the sergeant there."

Madeleine Muller

"I don't think we can wait till they arrive," Mila said.

"I know," Abongile replied, and Bonnie could feel his panic. There was no way he was going to stand and watch Mr Nel and his cronies push that car over the edge.

She wished she could tell him about the bullets.

Chapter 48: *Arno*

Arno was lying slumped back in the passenger seat of the Mercedes. He opened his eyes just enough to see what was going on outside.

Nobody was looking in their direction.

Mr Nel and the guard were busy unscrewing a last section of the fence - making a space big enough to scrape a car through. The whole crazy scenario was becoming way too real now.

Zola/ Indigo's reassuring silhouette was leaning on the front of the bonnet. Arno felt his heart beating in his ears. The whole thing was so extraordinarily impossible. He couldn't wait to get home and tell Jimmy. It was like he was in his very own Marvel movie. Except it wasn't a movie, and he sure as hell hoped that these superheroes knew what they were doing. They were still only a bunch of blerrie kids, after all, the same age as him.

Arno shivered. Lerato shifted next to him. He had also opened his eyes and was watching Mr Nel carefully. Arno had no doubt that the old man was itching to start the car and reverse out of there.

But they couldn't risk alerting Mr Nel. The man would be after them in a flash, and they wouldn't get far. Arno watched as the last bit of fence was hurled into the river and quickly closed his eyes as Mr Nel turned back towards them.

"Good work," the man said. "Let's get this car over this *verdompte*[86] ridge here. We are going to have to lift the front wheels of the car onto the pavement. Zola, is that handbrake still on?"

"Ja, *baas*. You want me to take it off?"

"Shush, Zola. Not so loud, man. What do you damn well think?" barked Mr Nel.

"*Uxolo*[87]…" Zola whispered and opened the driver's door. They leaned over Lerato to disengage the handbrake and whispered to them both.

"Abongile is almost here. He is coming via the rail track. Sit tight."

And then they were gone, slamming the door behind them. Arno hoped Abongile had backup. He suspected Mr Nel was not going to come easily.

Mr Nel and the other guard had taken position on each side of a front wheel, and Zola was stationed at the front.

"You guys ready?" Mr Nel asked, "On the count of three."

"One… Two… Three…"

Arno felt the car lift slightly and then heard Abongile's voice booming out over the bridge.

"Halt this minute. This is the police.…"

And then everything happened at once.

Mr Nel and the guard dropped the car, and the Mercedes banged down with a lurch. The momentum set it in motion, and the car started rolling slowly backwards.

The guard that had been helping Mr Nel with the fence didn't even look back. He just started legging it down the road towards the Free State border.

Mr Nel grabbed his revolver from beneath his jacket and ran towards his vehicle. He was behind the wheel within a split second. Indigo got into the passenger sheet of Mr Nel's car, and Arno's heart lurched.

What were they doing?

But perhaps it would be more dangerous if Indigo suddenly turned against Mr Nel. He was probably being strategic by keeping the status quo.

---

[86] cursed

[87] sorry

Superheroes in Sterkstroom

Arno looked back at Abongile. He was semi-crouched in the road, keeping the Mercedes between himself and the Hilux. Arno realised with shock that the ranger was not armed. He suspected Green Scorpions did not wear guns on their usual routine outrides. And where were Mila and Bonnie?

Lerato started the car and was about to drive off.

"Wait!" Arno said, "Abongile needs cover."

Lerato shook his head angrily, "You mean we should catch the bullets aimed at him?"

Arno looked back at the Hilux, which was now reversing and watched with horror as Mr Nel pointed his gun out of the open passenger window. Indigo was sitting upright, pressed back on the seat, and well out of the gun's sight. Arno made eye contact with them, and Indigo winked.

What the heck?

Arno watched Mr Nel pull the trigger and waited for the bang. But nothing happened. He tried again, and Arno could see his anger and frustration build as the gun didn't fire. Swearing, he threw the gun onto Indigo's lap, and Arno heard the squeal of tires as the Hilux took off.

He is getting away!

Madeleine Muller

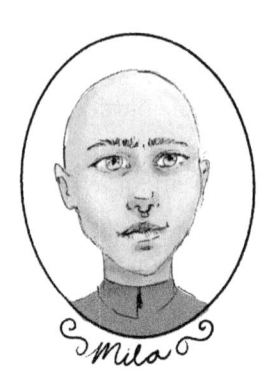

Chapter 49: *Mila*

Mila and Bonnie had tried to come up with various reasons why they accompany Abongile, but he was not having any of it. Mila had noticed with concern that he didn't even have a gun and wondered what he thought he was going to do when he got there. Abongile set off with a grim expression. The railway track running parallel to the road over the bridge was shrouded in darkness, and Abongile ducked down in the shadows. The twins waited for him to be a couple of hundred metres down the track before following him. Abongile had taken Mila's binoculars, so she was unable to track the events on the bridge from so far away. Mila had to get closer. She was the backup, after all. If things went wrong, it would be up to her to intervene.

As soon as they heard Abongile shout, they started running and got to the middle of the bridge as Mr Nel started up the Hilux and spun the wheels as he sped down the bridge towards the Free State border.

And Indigo was in the car beside him.
Why did they get in the car? This was crazy!
Mila shook her head once and closed her fist.

"Stop."

The world went quiet.

Superheroes in Sterkstroom

Mila stopped dead in her tracks and put her hands over her face, hot tears welling up. Bonnie was with her in an instant, her hand on Mila's shoulder.

"Indigo is fine, Mila. It was probably safer to get in the car and keep up the ruse. Everything is fine."

Mila nodded and wiped her eyes dry. The shock of watching that evil man drive off with Indigo beside him had caught her off guard. She took a couple of deep breaths. Bonnie was looking at her kindly.

"So what's the plan, sis?"

Mila smiled, "Turns out that Mr Nel is going to have a rather unfortunate breakdown in the middle of his getaway."

"Do you know how to disable a car with the engine running? I am guessing not quite as easy as emptying bullets from a gun," Bonnie said with concern. "We don't want to cause an accident…."

Mila nodded, "I'll ask Indigo. You better go and check what is happening at the Mercedes. Abongile seems to be in some sort of altercation with Lerato."

Mila jogged to the Hilux a hundred metres or so down the road. Indigo hardly blinked when Mila woke them up. It looked like they were enjoying Mila's unexpected arrivals.

"What the hell were you thinking?" Mila asked as Indigo climbed out of the car, shock and worry bubbling to the surface.

Indigo shrugged, "Wasn't really. Just going with the flow. And didn't want the bastard getting away. Where were you two?"

"Abongile wouldn't let us come. We had to lag behind. I got here just in time to see the two of you racing off."

"Aah. You worried about me?" Indigo said with a smirk, and Mila realised with embarrassment that they were flirting. Best to change the topic.

"I'm going to disconnect the battery whilst we are in fake time. When we get started again, the car will suddenly cut out and give Abongile time to catch up."

Indigo gave a small frown, "Good idea, but that might not work with a diesel engine. Safer to dislodge the fuel line. Pop that bonnet for me, and I'll sort it out."

Mila looked at Indigo with admiration as they quickly disabled the engine. They also needed to figure out how to get Indigo out of the way.

"And what is your plan?" Mila asked, "I don't think Abongile should get a close look at you."

Bonnie had caught up with them. She was laughing, "From what I can tell from that little tableau and little gentle mind reading, is that as soon as Mr Nel sped off, Abongile ran to the Mercedes and was quite surprised to find Lerato and Arno wide awake. He wanted to use the Mercedes to follow Mr Nel, but he and Lerato are arguing about who will drive…." Now that the worst of the danger was over, Bonnie was starting to enjoy the spectacle.

"Well," Mila said, "Abongile is not even looking in this direction. I think we can give Mr Nel a bit of a shock, hey Bonnie?"

Bonnie nodded knowingly and gave Mila a thumbs up.

Indigo looked at Mila with a raised eyebrow.

"Ok, you wicked witches. What's the plan?"

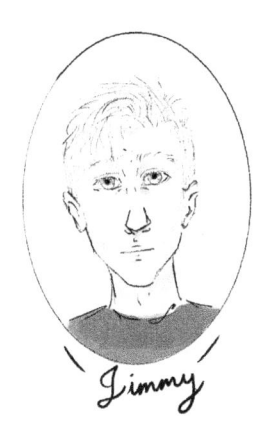

Chapter 50: *Jimmy*

It was a couple of hours past midnight when Jimmy and Ryan stumbled back into the rondawel. Ryan fell asleep on the couch, but Jimmy was revved up and wide awake. The youths had spent a tense couple of hours relaying messages using the radio at Mrs Braithwaite's, but once Arno and Lerato were rescued, they were no longer needed. Abongile had instructed Jimmy not to return to his own room in case Dr Kuzmich was still looking for him. The cops were on their way to come and arrest the old crook.

Arno and Lerato were fine, Jimmy told himself, still unable to believe it. When Abongile had called, he had specifically asked to speak to Jimmy to reassure him that Arno was unharmed. They had caught the kidnapper, although Abongile called the guy a 'mad man,' whatever that meant. The Ventersdorp cops were assisting, and they were all heading back to the police station to make statements and do, as Abongile called it, " a whole lot of bloody paperwork."

Jimmy's phone rang, and Ryan woke with a start. It was Mr Brandt. Ryan raised his eyebrows when Jimmy showed him his phone screen. "Sound sleepy, bra. And surprised," Ryan said, pretty sleepy himself.

"Hi, Dad. What's wrong?" Jimmy asked.

"What the hell happened, Jimmy? Did you know Arno had gone out?"

Madeleine Muller

Jimmy and Ryan had spent half the evening concocting a story, so Jimmy was ready. He put on a guilty voice,

"Ja, Dad. He was hanging out with some of those Green Scorpion kids. He is not even back yet. Is everything ok?"

Jimmy heard Mr Brandt's voice break and only then realised how upset his father was, "No, Jimmy. Arno was with Lerato, and the two got highjacked or something. In the Merc. But it's ok. They've been rescued, and they are both fine. The cops caught the guys at the Hennie Stein Bridge."

Ryan was making interesting facial expressions, demonstrating the level of upsetness Jimmy should portray in reply, but Jimmy did not have to pretend. Just thinking about Arno tied up in the back of that car made him want to vomit.

"Oh no, Dad! That can't be! What were they doing there?"

"I don't know, son. I don't know. It's all so unbelievable. And Abongile said I was not to say anything to Dr Kuzmich till he got back...."

Jimmy took the gap, "Dr Kuzmich was acting very strangely tonight, Dad. After that phone call, remember? But what would he have to do with it?"

"I don't know. I don't know," was all Mr Brandt said, over and over again. He sounded lost and confused, and Jimmy felt relieved. No, his dad definitely did not know anything about the plot tonight.

"I'll come to your room, Dad. We can go to Venterdorp together and go and fetch them."

Mr Brandt sighed, "We don't have a car, son."

"Mrs Braithwaite will help," Jimmy said and made a mental note to send Ryan to Mrs Braithwaite to ask her not to mention his involvement with the radio, "And Dad, I think we are going to have to come clean to the police about this plan for Mpangwa. Especially if Dr Kuzmich is involved...."

"Ja, ja. Sure, son," Mr Brandt said, clearly still in a daze. For the first time in his life, Jimmy felt in charge. He was the one who knew what was going on and what needed to be done.

And what he needed to do was go and fetch Arno.

Superheroes in Sterkstroom

Chapter 51: *Nina*

Nina was at Mpangwa reserve, out in the veldt. She was alone near the dam where they had been earlier that day.

But everything was different.

The veldt and the bush were lush as if it was the height of summer after lots of rain. The wild dagga was in full orange bloom, and the air was filled with sounds - good sounds. Chirping crickets and cicadas, singing frogs and chattering birds. At first, she couldn't see any animals, but there was a sudden rustle in the bush - and out popped her shrub hare - nibbling on some grass and looking around furtively. She looked to her left, and there were some impala, peacefully grazing with a family of warthogs snuffling behind them.

All was well…

Nina woke with a start and saw Patience's large and friendly face above her.

"Sorry, little one. It's 8.00 a.m. now. Time to test your sugar. I'm about to go off duty."

It had been a restless night. Nina had been woken every hour to have her finger pricked for the blood sugar test, and the fluid and dosing of insulin were adjusted accordingly. Apparently, her sugar had come down nicely, as well as something called ketones. Nina did not quite understand what ketones were, but she knew that she would only be discharged once they were all gone.

The quicker, the better.

Tess and Alex had returned to Mpangwa sometime in the middle of the night, and Nina wondered anxiously when they would be back. She wanted to tell Tess about her dream.

And at that very moment, Tess pulled back the curtains, Ryan peering over her shoulder.

"How's my sweet one?" Tess asked with a massive grin.

"Hah, hah. Very funny," Nina said.

Patience tutted and shook her head, "Visiting time is only at 11.00 a.m., but there has been some drama with one of your friends, so we are allowing Tess and Ryan to come and catch you up. They didn't want you to worry."

Patience gave them a warning frown and then set off.

Tess came to the side of the bed and was about to take Nina's hand, but Ryan pushed her aside and flung his arms around Nina's neck.

"I always said you were too sweet, hey. But this is taking it too far, girl."

Nina smiled. It had only been eight hours since she had discovered that her life had changed forever, but the shock was wearing off. What could you do?

"Apparently, no chocolate for me anymore…." Nina said. Ryan shook his head vehemently.

"No way! You can't live without chocolate. Isn't that like a major food group?"

"It is in your life," Tess commented drily, "But stop kidding around. We don't have much time."

Nina sat upright. She felt much stronger this morning than she had in days - just dreadfully thirsty. But that could wait….

"What happened? Did someone get hurt?"

"Everyone's fine," Tess said, "We wanted to let you know that they found the cause of that sound. Mr Kuzmich had invented a piece of rather horrid machinery that creates this high-pitched noise, only detected by animals. It was set up in a bunker at the bottom of an old reservoir, and he had hired a security company to keep an eye on it at night."

"Arno found it," Ryan announced proudly.

"Ja, except then he got caught by Mr Nel, the security company guy. And his chauffeur, *nogal*! Bonnie, Mila and Indigo saved the day, but we haven't heard the whole story yet. After Mr Nel and Dr Kuzmich were arrested and all nicely locked up, Abongile and Mr Dyani went and disabled the machine. And Indigo and the twins went back into the bush and sorted out all the animals. They only got back like a couple of hours ago and were completely wiped. They promised to come later and fill us in on all the details. So everything is fine now...."

Ryan put his hand up, "Can I tell her about Mr Nel? Please let me tell her about Mr Nel."

Tess rolled her eyes, "Why do you put your hand up like that, Ryan? Geez. I'm not a school teacher."

Nina laughed, "Please, Ryan. Do tell about Mr Nel."

"Ok, picture this, right. Abongile arrives on the scene...."

"He caught up with them at the Hennie Steyn bridge. Did you know that it is the longest bridge in South Africa....?" Tess added unnecessarily.

Ryan glared at her and continued, "Mr Nel jumps in his fancy-pantsy car and drives off with Indigo in the passenger seat...."

"Indigo is in the shape of one of his guards. But Mr Nel doesn't know this...." Tess interjected.

"Anyways, Mr Nel is driving off at great speed when suddenly the guard next to him... *disappears*...." Ryan accentuated 'disappears' with a dramatic magician movement of the hands, "...into thin air."

"And the engine splutters a couple of times and comes to a complete standstill," Tess said gleefully.

Ryan had laid himself crossways over the bottom of Nina's bed, holding his stomach in laughter. He then sat bolt upright to complete the tale, "When Abongile got to the car, Mr Nel was in such shock he didn't even protest when Abongile cuffed him. He kept on muttering, "Zola, where the hell is Zola?"

"Who is Zola?" Nina asked.

"Oh, that was Indigo's isiXhosa name for the guard they were pretending to be. And the best is that both Lerato and Arno swore they didn't know what Mr Nel was talking about. That they had not seen this Zola person. So Mr Nel thinks he is going crazy or something."

Nina smiled, "That was Mila, hey? Doing her magic."

Ryan nodded, "Like that time with Barry[88]. Indigo got out of the car whilst Mila had frozen time and made themself scarce after they disabled the engine. So when Mila unfreeze time, the car died and … Poof. Indigo gone. Geez, I wish I could have been there."

"Ryan and Jimmy handled communications at base camp," Tess added, " and got Abongile and the Ventersdorp police to that bridge in time."

Nina smiled and lay back on the cushions. She was suddenly very tired. "I had this dream, Tess, about the animals. That they were all awake and that everything was fine. And to be honest, I am quite glad I missed out on all the action. I'm just happy that it was all sorted out."

"Eish. And the action is only just beginning. Mr Nel was so freaked out that he was squealing like a baby and had no problem selling out Dr Kuzmich. And Mila told us that Mr Brandt tried to punch Dr Kuzmich when they brought him into the police station. Mr Brandt and Jimmy were there to pick up Arno."

"I'm glad Jimmy's dad wasn't involved. That would have been horrible," Nina said and closed her eyes.

"We'll go now. Alex is chatting with the doctors and will come and say hi in a bit. And Granny Jenni and Maria will be here by eleven for visiting time," Tess said, kissing her friend goodbye on the forehead.

As Tess left, Ryan came over and sat down on the bed. Nina opened her eyes and looked at him weakly.

"You're going to be ok, hey my *Nina Karenina?*"

Nina nodded, "Sure, Ryan, I'll be fine."

"Even without chocolate?" Ryan asked, and Nina wanted to giggle at his seriousness.

"They do make diabetic chocolate, Ryan."

---

[88] See 'Dimbaza Divine'

Superheroes in Sterkstroom

"Really, hey? Cool bananas. That's ok, then. Love you, my girl." And with a wave, he was off.

Madeleine Muller

Chapter 52: *Arno*

Arno opened his eyes at the smell of freshly brewed coffee. He had collapsed into bed when they got in at 4.00 a.m. that morning, fully dressed, and felt like he had slept half the day away. He checked his watch. It was 2.00 p.m. The curtains were closed, and the room was deliciously cool. Arno looked across at the other twin bed, which was neatly made up. With a start, he sat up, suddenly alarmed. *Where was Jimmy?*

But Jimmy was standing at the end of the bed with a tray of coffee and rusks.

They had hardly spoken when Mr Brandt and Jimmy had arrived at the Ventersdorp police station. Jimmy had looked like he wanted to say something, but Mr Brandt had grabbed Arno into a large bear hug and burst into tears. And then there were forms to sign, explanations to make, and they had to sort out how to get the Mercedes back, which was supposedly now part of the evidence.

And then there was the moment when the cops arrived with Dr Kuzmich, his hands handcuffed in front of him… Jimmy's dad had jumped up and almost whacked him one. Arno suspected Abongile had anticipated trouble because he was up in a flash, holding Marthinus Brandt's back firmly.

Superheroes in Sterkstroom

"Don't worry, Mr Brandt. Igor Kuzmich will get what's coming to him," he had said softly in the angry man's ear.

When all the procedures had been completed, Abongile had driven them back to the reserve with Mr Brandt sitting in the front and Lerato, Arno and Jimmy in the back seat. The two young men couldn't catch up with so many people in the car, but when they turned into the Mpangwa Reserve gate, Jimmy quietly took Arno's hand, and they sat like that all the way back - Arno feeling almost more anxious than he did when he had been caught. But this was good anxiety.

Mr Brandt had walked them back to the rondawel, checking that the locks on all the doors worked and carefully closing all the windows. Arno had never seen Mr Brandt so vulnerable before. It was a good look on him.

Arno had vaguely thought about a shower before turning in but decided just to lie down for a little bit before brushing his teeth…

*

"Good morning. Do you know that you still have two ponytails on the top of your head?" Jimmy was smiling as he said this.

Arno patted the top of his head and smiled as he pulled out the elastics and ran his hands through his hair, "Ja, hey. It's my new badass look." *He must look like hell.*

"You look surprisingly great," Jimmy said as if he were reading his mind, "like Indiana Jones after a particularly rough night in the jungle."

Arno sat up, and Jimmy came over and placed a tray on his lap.

"Got you some proper coffee in the main house. Better drink it while it's hot. And some of Mrs Braithwaite's homemade rusks. She sends her best, by the way. Nyama has made a miraculous recovery. You and Lerato are the local celebrities now."

Arno's eyes widened, "How come?"

Jimmy laughed, "Because of our brilliant press agent, Ryan the Lion. That guy does not shut up."

"You better tell me what he said. We will need to get our stories straight."

Jimmy shrugged, "It's all mostly true. The story is that you and Lerato went on a little night hike, all innocent-like, and stumbled *by accident* on the reservoir with Dr Kuzmich's evil machine. The rest is pretty much true. The two of you got caught by Mr Nel, who tried to push the two of you, trapped in the Mercedes, off the Hennie Stein Bridge. In the meantime, Indigo and the twins had gone looking for you when you didn't come back and had picked up the Hilux and Mercedes when they left Mpangwa and decided to follow it. And, of course, Ryan was the radio controller that informed Abongile and the cops."

"But what about you?" Arno protested, "I thought the radio was all your idea?"

Jimmy shook his head, "I told Ryan and Mrs Braithwaite to please leave me out of it. It's too complicated with my dad. He is all torn up as it is. If he knew that I was part of the whole rescue mission and had not involved him… That would not be good."

Arno dunked his rusk and bit off a large chunk, carefully positioning the rusk over his cup.

"Oh, boy. Do I have stuff to tell you. Stuff you won't believe."

Jimmy nodded enthusiastically, "Ryan told me that your new friends have got some rather spectacular skills. At first, I was a bit alarmed at the idea of only a bunch of teenagers out on your rescue mission. I thought Ryan was making up stories just to make me feel better. But then the twins were sending all these messages via the geo app…." Jimmy made himself comfortable on the side of the bed, "But we didn't get the details of exactly what happened last night, as Indigo and the twins had to go off and shut down that horrible machine or something. I want to hear all about it."

Arno moved over to give Jimmy more space and looked at his friend in amazement. Something had changed. There was none of the usual insecurity and worry that usually surrounded Jimmy. It was like he had grown up overnight and become his own man.

"What happened to you last night?" Arno said, "You're different, a good different, I mean. But different."

Jimmy looked Arno in the eyes, "I guess I finally realised who I was and what was important to me."

Arno's heart began to beat faster. Was he getting this straight? Was Jimmy talking about him? And what did that mean?

Jimmy looked at Arno a little bit longer as if trying to read what was in his mind.

And then he leaned forward and kissed him.

A slow lingering kiss. Quiet and real.

Jimmy sat back and looked at Arno, "Is this ok?"

Arno's whole body tingled, and he could feel his face heating up.

"Since when do you kiss boys?" he asked with a smile.

"Since I found one I really like," Jimmy said and then repeated, this time a bit less sure, "Is this ok?"

"You bet…." Arno said and pulled him closer.

The story of his superhero rescue could wait.

Madeleine Muller

Indigo

Chapter 53: Indigo

It was 3.00 p.m. and visiting time at the Sterkstroom District Hospital. There were seven of them around Nina's bed, and Nomsa, the nurse, who had taken over the day shift, was making a fuss.

"Hayi! This is supposed to be a high-care bed. If it was COVID, we wouldn't even have more than one guest in here at a time."

"Ja, Auntie," Ryan said, "But these are special circumstances. And there's no more COVID *mos*. We are all vaccinated, boosted and what not."

Indigo felt vaguely like an imposter, but only if ne gave it a moment's thought. Being here amongst these people was like being amongst family. Mila had found chairs for Granny Jenny and Maria and the head of the bed, with granny holding Nina's left hand, the one without the infusion line. Ryan and Tess were each sitting on the side of the bed, both looking like they needed a good night's sleep. Indigo, Mila and Bonnie were standing at the bottom.

Like three guardian angels, Indigo thought.

"Oh, my dear Nina," Granny Jenni was saying, "The doctor says that he thinks you will be able to come home in a couple of days, but we might have to go and spend a few days in East London to get trained up."

"Trained up?" Ryan asked, "Like on where to get diabetic chocolate?"

Superheroes in Sterkstroom

Jenni nodded, "Exactly, dear Ryan. We will meet with a diabetic nurse to teach us about injections and sugar testing, and a dietician to teach us about what Nina can eat, and yes, Ryan, where to get diabetic chocolate. And we will find a nice doctor to help with monitoring Nina's progress."

"Geez. It sounds like a lot of work," Ryan said, sounding worried.

"But it will keep Nina alive," Tess said, sounding a bit gruffer than she probably meant to. Everyone was strained to the max with all the events over the last two days, but mostly owing to their worry for this extraordinary child.

"Well, I am glad you are looking so much better, Nina," Mila said. You gave us a hell of a fright."

Bonnie nodded but looked pale and concerned. Indigo knew that if Bonnie could find some sort of way to blame herself, she would do so.

Mila turned to Indigo, "We should probably thin out the crowd around this bed a bit. I'm thirsty. Want to join me for a cheap Twizza outside on the pavement?"

"Sure," Indigo agreed, "Now there's an offer a dude can't resist."

It was pleasant outside in the sunshine, with clear skies overhead. The worst of the day's heat had settled down, and the earlier crowds queuing to get into the hospital had thinned out. It was mostly people waiting for taxis to take them home, and there was the gentle hum of chatter around the pavement: food stalls stocked with apples, sweets and even a *tshisha nyama*[89].

"Nice place, old Sterkstroom, " Indigo said mostly to make conversation, although it was indeed a quaint old town with broad streets and antiquated houses down the main road.

"Ja," Mila huffed, "if you like small towns. I think I am more of a city girl."

"Is that where you are heading next year? To the city? Bonnie mentioned you guys might take a gap year."

Mila shrugged, "Maybe."

Indigo decided to take a risk, "Durban, I assume?"

Mila raised her eyebrows, "And why do you assume that?"

---

[89] Stall selling barbecued meat.

"Bonnie said something about a boyfriend? Some gorgeous Indian guy studying marine biology?"

Indigo was pleased to see that Mila looked uncomfortable. It was not often one saw Mila discomfited.

"Ja, sort of. I mean long distance relationships are the pits, right. And Anish is great. It's just. I don't know. He was the perfect first romance...."

"But not the last one...."

Mila smiled at this. "Nope. I guess not."

Indigo's heart began to beat a little faster. Did this mean ne was actually in the running?

Mila took another sip of her Twizza, "And you? What are your plans for next year?"

Indigo shrugged, "I'm definitely taking a gap year. Still need to figure out who I am and what I actually want to do with my life."

"It will be nothing ordinary, that's for sure," Mila said.

Indigo took a deep breath, "We should team up - Bonnie, you and I. I'm sure there is a whole lot of trouble we can get ourselves into."

Mila nodded, "I would like that," she said and looked down shyly.

If her skin wasn't so dark, she'd be blushing, Indigo thought. Mila suddenly looked like the seventeen-year-old teenager she was.

"Want to go for a walk down High Street?" Indigo asked and put out nir hand. There was not much else on offer in Sterkstroom.

Mila looked a little surprised but took Indigo's hand without hesitation and smiled.

"Sure. Going to be a short walk, though."

Indigo laughed and felt nir heart lift. Ne had been hoping to find at least one other like nem in the world, but instead, ne had found not only a whole bunch of friends but perhaps even love….

Epilogue

It was early morning, and Nina was sitting on the grass inside the chicken tractor with Captain Henry on her lap. Since returning home a couple of weeks ago, she had taken on a new appreciation for her happy, albeit not the brightest, fluffy-butt chickens.

Maggie, one of the younger chicks who was growing up fast, was trying to peck at the little white, round plastic devise seemingly stuck to Nina's outer arm.

"*Hiert*," Nina chased her off, "That's my Libre."

It was one of the small miracles of modern science and had been recommended by the lovely dietician that had been helping them figure out the best diet for Nina. The hardest bit of having diabetes, Nina had learnt, had been pricking her fingers to test her blood. The injections hardly hurt at all, and Nina had quickly learnt the knack of injecting herself. But the pricking was the worst - and she had to do blood sugar tests when she woke up, before every meal and whenever she did not feel well.

But the *Freestyle Libre* was a CGM (continuous glucose monitor) - a clever little device just a bit bigger than one of those old-fashioned coins. It had a small needle that was inserted just under Nina's skin and attached to her arm with a plaster. You only needed to replace it every two weeks, which meant no more pricking. Nina could simply scan the Libre with her phone, and it would give her a graph of her blood sugar levels over the last eight hours.

At first, Nina had hesitated to say yes to the Libre, worrying about the cost, but it turned out that all her insulin, as well as the Libre, were covered by their medical aid - another small miracle.

"Howzit, Nina Karenina!"

Nina looked up and saw Ryan sprinting over the lawn. It was as if Ryan had only two modes - super awake or fast asleep. Since her diagnosis, Ryan had been making an extra effort to help out. Nina was already feeling a lot better but still easily ran out of steam in the middle of trying to do something. And when her sugar levels were out, high or low, she felt sick and irritable.

Ryan opened the tractor's gate and stepped in, quickly closing it behind him before the chickens escaped.

"*More, more. En hoe is my hoenertjies?*[90]"

Nina smiled, "We are all fine, thank you. Although I am suspicious that Maggie might not be a Maggie after all, but a Martin."

Ryan shook his head, "No, man. That's the third chick that turned out to be a rooster. But maybe it's just a little identity crisis, hey?"

Nina shook her head, "Nope. He has definitely got the start of a nice knobbly comb."

"Eish. At least they can keep Captain Henry company on his nightly exile. Have you fed the monsters yet?"

"I've given them food. Just need to sort out the water."

"I'll do that," Ryan said and picked up the water container, a semi-transparent plastic cone upended on a red water dish, "And you, have you had brekfis, my girl?"

"Not yet," Nina admitted.

Ryan rubbed his hands together, "How about some bacon and fresh eggs, hey? I'll fry some up after I've filled the water."

The biggest change to Nina's diet had been cutting out all the sugar and processed carbs, but she had quickly figured out a few favourite meals that did not affect her sugar at all, bacon and eggs becoming a staple breakfast.

Nina got up, and Captain Henry fluttered down and gave Maggie, or rather, Martin, a quick chase around the coop. Life was pretty predictable in a chicken tractor!

Ryan fetched fresh water, and Nina collected the eggs laid the night before. Together they walked back towards the house. Nina would have to check her sugar levels and inject the insulin needed to cover any starch in her breakfast to ensure her sugar stayed at the right level.

"School starts again tomorrow," Ryan said.

"I'm a bit nervous," Nina admitted, "There is so much to keep track of with this stupid diabetes."

"We'll be ok," Ryan said matter of factly, "And I'll help."

---

[90] Morning, morning. And how are my chicks?

Nina smiled, "And how exactly will you be helping, Ryan?"

"Anyone offer you a chocolate or a sweetie or what not, and I'll disappear it…." Ryan clicked his fingers, "…like that."

Nina laughed and hooked her arm into Ryan's.

"Excellent idea, my friend. Whatever would I do without you?"

Madeleine Muller

Acknowledgments

There is a joy in meeting new characters and watching them develop, quite independently of any plans I may have laid down at the start. I therefore need to thank Indigo, Arno and Jimmy for their contributions, sometimes quite unexpected, to the plot!

But it is difficult to let go of old friends, and as a result my books are getting thicker and thicker. And this has implications. I can no longer hope to write two stories a year for each's of my children's birthdays!

Superheroes in Sterkstroom is therefore dedicated to both Ron and Benji for the year 2022 . You are the reasons why I write and my biggest inspiration.

In October 2020 our family has also had to meet the challenge of looking after a child with type 1 diabetes. It is through the support of family and friends that we are able to take on each new day. Thank you!

Thank you to the Emonti Creative circle with Jen Moorcroft for their support and encouragement and to Roxanne Phillips, my editor, who completed the editing of my second-language grammar in record time for Benji's birthday. I promise to give more notice next time… And to Athule Mabhali who helped me with the finer nuances of the IsiXhosa language.

Benji Muller did the illustrations and is able to imagine my characters better than I can. Thank you for meeting the deadlines during your final Matric exams!

And lastly thank you to Tom, the rock upon which I build everything.

Madeleine Muller

Superheroes in Sterkstroom

About the author

Madeleine Muller is a medical doctor, working as both a senior lecturer for Walter Sisulu University and as a Family Physician specialist at Cecilia Makiwane Hospital Family Medicine Department in Mdantsane, East London.

She has been writing youth novellas since 2013 and *Superheroes in Sterkstroom* is the fourth publication that follows the adventures of Mila and Bonnie.

She lives in Chintsa West, East London, South Africa with her husband, Tom, and her two teenage children.

November 2022

To contact Madeleine Muller and keep track of new publications:

Follow her on Instagram **@drmadmuller**

Printed in Great Britain
by Amazon